THE UNTAMEABLES

F.T. MARINETTI

THE

UNTAMEABLES

Translated from the Italian by
Jeremy Parzen
with an Introduction by
Luigi Ballerini

SUN &
MOON
CLASSICS
28

SUN & MOON PRESS
Los Angeles • 1994

Sun & Moon Press
Contemporary Arts Educational Project, Inc.
a nonprofit corporation
oulevard, Los Angeles, California 90036

ed in paperback in 1994 by Sun & Moon Press
9 8 7 6 5 4 3 2 1
FIRST EDITION
968 by Arnoldo Mondadori Editore
La Grande Milano tradizionale e futurista /
Una sensibilita italiana nata in Egitto
Copyright ©1969 El Libro S. A. Bellinzona
Copyright ©1969 Arnoldo Mondadori Editore
Translation Copyright ©1994 by Sun & Moon Press
Introduction Copyright ©1994 by Luigi Ballerini
Permission to retranslate *The Untameables* by
Farrar, Straus and Giroux, Inc., whose
Marinetti: Selected Writings contained a
translation of *The Untameables* by Arthur A. Coppotelli
Copyright ©1971, 1972 by Farrar, Straus and Giroux
All rights reserved

This book was made possible, in part, through an operational grant from the
Andrew W. Mellon Foundation, and through contributions to
The Contemporary Arts Educational Project, Inc.,
a nonprofit corporation

Cover: Umberto Boccioni, *Riot in the Galleria (Risa in Galleria)*, 1910
Cover and Design: Katie Messborn
Typography: Guy Bennett

LIBRARY OF CONGRESS CATALOGING IN PUBLICATION DATA
Marinetti, Filippo Tomamaso [1876–1944]
The Untameables
p. cm — (Sun & Moon Classics: 28)
ISBN: 1-55713-064-7
I. Title. II. Series.
811'.54—dc20

Printed in the United States of America on acid-free paper.

CONTENTS

ITALY AND/OR MARINETTI
FROM ALEXANDRIA TO VITTORIO VENETO

for the Jar and the dilemma of Lucky Son

Our journey begins in Alexandria: not because Filippo Tommaso Marinetti first saw the light in this Egyptian city, nor because Giuseppe Ungaretti, the occasional fellow-traveller of the Futurists, "burned with unawareness" on the embankments of the Lower Nile.[1] It begins there because of Constantine Cavafy, a Greek poet to whom the founder of the Futurist movement paid homage—moderate as it may have been—in his *Il fascino dell'Egitto* (*The Charm of Egypt*).[2]

Here, among other things, Marinetti states that Cavafy's demotic language "has a powerful vitality outside and against classical grammar."[3] The seemingly sympathetic tone of this observation, however, must not be construed as an index of compatibility: the notion of destroying the past, the keystone of the Futurist edifice, must have tasted to Cavafy like the castor oil that Italian Fascists so generously administered to their opponents.

Yet, it is with images extracted from his epiphanies that we intend to open the gate of the Futurist maze lying ahead. "What are we waiting for, assembled in the forum?"[4] asks Cavafy in a text rife with felicitous emblematic values. "The barbarians are due here today." This single answer is provided time and again to satisfy the curiosity of the bystander and to create a feeling of comfort. The incoming flux of questions, however, will soon make that comfort a short-lived experience:

Why isn't anything happening in the senate?
Why do the senators sit there without legislating?

Because the barbarians are coming today.
What laws can the senate make now?
Once the barbarians are here, they'll do the legislating…

and so on, until the final rude awakening:

Why this sudden restlessness, this confusion?
(How serious people's faces have become.)
Why are the streets and squares emptying so rapidly,
everyone going home so lost in thought?

> Because night has fallen and the barbarians have not come.
> And some who have just returned from the border say,
> there are no barbarians any longer.

> And now, what's going to happen to us without barbarians?
> They were, those people, a kind of solution.

Allegories have one "disadvantage": when the correspondence is established between their meaning and the idea to which that meaning applies, they may end up signifying more than one bargained for. The fear of unexpected consequences, however, did not stop us from postulating that the equations *Barbarians = Futurists* and *a kind of solution = Futurist aesthetics* are plausible and perhaps even desirable. Moreover, we have embraced the ironic complication implied in the locution *a kind of*.

From this alignment there surfaces a thought, or better yet, a diachronic corollary to Cavafy's text that may prove to be even more disturbing than the poem's open-ended conclusion. The Barbarians have indeed arrived, but they have lost the sense of their special identity: they themselves mingle unnoticed in the crowd and ask the question, "Why this sudden restlessness, this confusion?...Why are the streets and squares emptying so rapidly...?" A second, equally fertile instigation reads as follows: the Barbarians have not ceased to be, but the forms of their expression have become all-pervasive and have shortcircuited the epochal function of their innovations.

In this perspective, the inquiry about the Barbarians' "non-arrival" does not have to be viewed as a prelude to catastrophe. In fact, it opens pathways that lead beyond the negative pleasures of rationalization. "Waiting for a solution" no longer means idly biding time and vegetating in the obsession that prevents thought from becoming deed. It means, instead, entering the special frame of mind necessary for artistic creation. "Waiting" becomes the opportunity for consciousness to produce its own morphology. In this case, the concepts commonly used to characterize "waiting" (such as length, duration, and sequential development) are replaced with tension, alertness and excitment. Unlike apples on a tree that are ripened by the passing of the seasons, the human being's maturation is generated from inside. It is not time that causes him to mature; it is he that lives to cause time to "fulfill its promise." This can only occur when knowledge and wisdom burgeon from the experience of making things rather than from the expectations of pre-ordained and rationally constructed theories.[5]

Seldom do atemporal or de-temporalized forms of "waiting" penetrate Futurist writing so significantly as they do in *The Untameables*.[6] This quasi-novel[7] extols art as the activity that can redeem the human experience from the *Zeitgeist* imposed upon it by politics. This redemption is inherent in the divergent use that art and politics make of history. Art produces new syntagms out of its own history, and it does so by contradicting the very paradigms upon which that history is founded. In other words, art wages a constant war against history: it deploys an oneiric grammar that disengages it from the linear configurations of time. Politics, on the other hand, engages time, impressing upon it the rhythm of its own mechanisms. It believes in measures, just like logic. It turns predictions into paradigms and serves as the clock of the future. While art subtracts itself from time, politics needs time to produce the illusion of progress.

Never before had Marinetti shown any propensity to accept, let alone to endorse, a philosophy that so categorically separated the effects of art and politics. Everything he wrote prior to *The Untameables* would seem to indicate that he believed in exactly the opposite. For Marinetti politics was not just the sectorial application of a given ideology; it involved the human being's totality and resulted naturally from the equation *life = art*.

This maxim was never fully comprehended nor accepted by the non-Futurist members of the fledgeling Fascist Movement which Marinetti had pratically cofounded with Mussolini in 1919.[8] After the crushing defeat of the Fascists in the elections of the same year and the reorganization of their party, it became apparent to Marinetti that Mussolini was leading Fascism down a reactionary path wholly incongruous with the avant-garde ideals of Futurism. The recognition of this fundamental disparity led Marinetti to resign from the *Fasci di combattimento*.[9]

In light of this courageous decision, his later reconciliation with Mussolini constitutes a desperate compromise and a blatant contradiction of his aesthetic propensities. Marinetti's interpretation of Mussolinian politics as the partial realization of the Futurist program was an act of surrender that stifled whatever aesthetic energy was left in the movement after WWI.

With Vittorio Veneto[10] and the Fascists' rise to power, the Futurist minimal program has been fulfilled.

This minimal program championed Italian pride, unlimited faith in the future of Italian people, the destruction of the Austrian-Hungarian Empire, daily heroics, the love of danger, the rehabilitation of violence as the deciding factor of all disputes, the religion of velocity, of innovation, of optimism, and of originality, young people's rise to power against parliamentary, bureaucratic, academic and pessimistic spirit.

Italian Futurism, which is characterized by patriotism, has generated a large number of foreign Futurist movements, but it has nothing in common with their political policies, like the Bolshevik policy of Russian Futurism which has become nothing more than state art.[11]

Futurists and Fascists could certainly find a limited number of convergent points, but the diametrical opposition of their artistic philosophies made that convergence fruitless and downright absurd. The Fascists were not ready to consider avant-garde art as an essential feature of the human experience and could, at best, tolerate it as an *instrumentum regni*. On the other hand, Marinetti's occasional criticism levelled at forms of art enslaved by *raison d'etat* (as in the passage cited above) could hardly be seen as a guarantee that, under the aegis of Fascism, Italian Futurism would maintain the autonomy and purity of its origins. The patriotic sentiment shared by both Fascists and Futurists gave rise not only to symbiotic assimilations, but also a number of dangerous misunderstandings:

> ...Fascism contains and will always contain that bulk of proud, violent, insolent, and war-like patriotism that we Futurists, first and foremost, preached to the Italian masses. For this reason we *strenuously support Fascism*...Fascism functions in a political capacity...
>
> Futurism functions instead in the infinite dominion of pure imagination, so it can and must dare dare dare ever more recklessly.[12]

The Futurists paid dearly for their "strenuous support." They were looking for aesthetic freedom, but all they got was political protection. In order to fit the Fas-

cist mold, their notion of patriotism had to be slimmed
down considerably. Next to the optimism, pride, violence,
bullyness and the war-like spirit of Fascist patriotism,
we no longer find the concepts of artistic ingenuity and
creativity that so conspicuously characterized Futurist
patriotism at the time of *The Founding Manifesto* and in
the years of the Great War. Fascist patriotism left Futurist imagination little or no room to "dare."

The notion of art as an all-encompassing manifesta-
tion of life (and thus also of politics) began to lose its
power of persuasion. At the same time, the old academic
distinction between theory and praxis was restored, and
art was once again paraded in the paddock of marginal
and ultimately unnecessary activities. The downscaling
of Futurist ambitions brought about an uncanny synec-
dochic reversal: Fascism, the part, subsumed the Futurist movement which only a few years earlier had regarded itself as the whole. Inevitably, the frequent declaration of primogeniture made by Marinetti sounded
like the symptomatic refrain of a man suffering from
delusions of grandeur: the more assertive he became,
the more illusory his claim appeared to be.

The Futurist Political Manifesto, authored by
Marinetti before the end of the war in 1918, lay inertly
on the table of Italian politics, while the Fascist program, which had assimilated a good many points from
the earlier charter, became "the law of the land." Futurism began to belittle itself by assigning the epithet "ar-

tistic" to any political or military endeavor carried out by the Fascists, and Marinetti eventually died a staunch advocate of the Republic of Salò.[13]

The rigid dynamics of Marinetti's political predicament appear to be in strident contrast with the short-lived, yet unequivocal aesthetic intuition that guided his work during his absence from political life (in particular, 1922, the year of *The Untameables* and the March on Rome). An indication of this contrast may be inferred by contextualizing the catchphrase "L'Italia di Vittorio Veneto."

By that time, the expression had become a slogan of indignation and vindication. It captured the victorious spirit that had pervaded the nation at the conclusion of World War I, a spirit largely neglected, in both domestic and foreign policy, by the weak politicians who governed the country in the aftermath. Both Marinetti and Mussolini appropriated it to suit their inherently irreconcilable *agenda*.

Charged with the task of forming a new government, the Fascist leader used the phrase to impress upon King Victor Emanuel III[14] that the era of political compromise was over: Fascism would galvanize the country by empowering those—or some of those—who had defeated Austria and the central powers.

Marinetti certainly agreed with the Duce on this particular point, but his use of the phrase reflects a strictly Futuristic position for which the Fascists showed hardly any interest. The expression appears twice in the preface to *The Untameables*.[15] In the first instance, he used it to assert that the free-word compositional technique, which he claimed to have employed in his book, was becoming the matrix of a national style:

> Our words in freedom give birth to the new synthesized Italian style, rapid, simultaneous, incisive, the new style completely freed from all the classical frills and robes, *a style capable of wholly expressing the souls of the ultrarapid victors at Vittorio Veneto*.[16]

In the second instance, it concludes a less focused line of reasoning which claims, nonetheless, another victory for Futurist aesthetics:

> The great Futurist decorative art has been realized. In Rome, yes, in Rome, which could not continue to be the sole fortress of traditionalism. Rome is becoming the capital of the new Italy of Vittorio Veneto; it is becoming and will become more and more as the power plant of world Futurism.[17]

Was Marinetti planning his own March on Rome? Not quite. His tactics, however, if not his convictions, were beginning to change, and they would eventually take a course for which *The Untameables* had not prepared us. This "outlandish" narrative clearly separates the before and the after of its author's career. When, years later, Marinetti descended upon Rome, he did not do so, really, as an avant-garde poet, but as a pathetically anaesthetized member of the Accademia d'Italia.[18] Had the conflict between Futurist art and Fascism continued, it would have denied Fascism their most supple artistic alibi and given Futurism a second chance to fructify.

Given the pivotal importance of *The Untameables*, it is astonishing that the book has not received the kind of critical attention it deserves. Except for the observations made by Luciano De Maria in the introduction to *Teoria e invenzione futurista*, contemporary criticism— by and large—has chosen to ignore the anomaly this book represents in the trajectory of Marinetti's career.[19] This neglect may be explained, at least in part, by the fact that the plot is decidedly bizarre. Furthermore, none of the more audacious tenets of Futurist writing seem to have had any desire to show themselves prominently in these pages, even though Marinetti states otherwise in his prefatory avocation.

What we have, instead, is a return to the hyperbolic style of Marinetti's African themes. This affords us the opportunity to regard *The Untameables* as a transparent testimonial of the aesthetic and political restlessness he must have experienced when Fascism was becoming the dominant feature of Italian life. The shaky foundation of the book's formal structure may indeed confirm and perhaps even expand this supposition. It would be difficult, however, to reach any mature conclusion without first drafting a survey of the rhetorical strategies utilized in Marinetti's overtly avant-garde writings.

*

The theory of a substantial dichotomy between Marinetti's early writings and his "truly" Futurist works must be discarded on account of their thematic and stylistic continuity.[20] In spite of this fact, no one has dared to suggest that the birth of Futurism be antedated. On February 20, 1909, as it is well known, *The Founding Manifesto* appeared for the first time on the front page of the Parisian daily *Le Figaro*. The major difference between the two phases in Marinetti's career is the taxonomic fury that overcame him and the Futurists when they sought to lay out the normative principles of their enterprise.

The Founding Manifesto[21] oscillates between a clearly defined set of aesthetic prescriptions and a loosely knit narrative aimed at historical contextualization and outright myth-making.

The notorious eleven commandments of Futurism[22] constitute a modern version of the topos "I bring things never said before."[23] It is no surprise to see it harbored in a document devoted to the promise of a post-humanistic world which heralds not the "unexpected" but simply the "not-yet-experienced."

Traditionally, a topos of this sort belongs in the *exordium*; Marinetti instead chose to sandwich it between a narrative and an exhortation. In the former, which marks the opening of the manifesto, Marinetti reverses the humble tones of the *captatio benevolentiae* and replaces them with the arrogance of solitude. It is an attempt to derive pleasure from a radical distillation of contrasts and the forswearing of conventional discourse:

> We had stayed up all night, my friends and I...An immense pride was buoying us up, because we felt ourselves alone at that hour, alone, awake, and on our feet, like proud beacons or forward sentries against an army of hostile stars glaring down at us from their celestial encampments. Alone with the stokers feeding the hellish fires of great ships, alone with the black specters who grope in the red-hot bellies of locomotives launched down their crazy courses, alone with the drunkards reeling like wounded birds along city walls.[24]

In the exhortation, Marinetti unashamedly adopts the very tones rejected in the narrative and concludes the manifesto with a direct appeal to the emotions of an ideal reader:

> It is from Italy that we launch through the world this violently upsetting, incendiary manifesto...For too long has Italy been a dealer in second hand clothes. We mean to free

her from the numberless museums that cover her like so
many graveyards...

The oldest of us is thirty...When we are forty, other
younger and stronger men will throw us in the waste basket,
like useless manuscripts ——we want it to happen![25]

In *Let's Murder the Moonshine*, published a few
months after *The Founding Manifesto*, a number of
Marinetti's favorite themes (war, death, carnage, orgy,
conquest, exaltation of madness and the mechaniza-
tion of nature) are curiously cast in narrative form. Here
too, as in so many other manifestos which the Futurists
relentlessly produced well into the 1930s, it is impossible to clearly extricate scientific and didactic registers from purely narrative modes.

Be it strictly grammatical or broadly hortatory, any
given manifesto can be the vehicle for political ideology: at times the message is clearly spelled out; at times
it emerges from considerations that seem to have little
to do with politics.

The most revealing example of this *mesaillance* is
the *Manifesto of the Italian Futurist Party* of 1918, but
this ideology and the accompanying propagandistic at-
titude had already surfaced in a number of seemingly
unrelated manifestos.

Take, for instance, the opening statement of *Futurist
Cinema* (1916):

The book, a wholly passéist[26] means of preserving and communicating thought, has been doomed for a long time to disappear, along with cathedrals, towers, gables, museums and pacifist idealism. The book, this static companion of the sedentary, the nostalgic, the neutralist,[27] cannot amuse or exalt the new Futurist generations intoxicated with revolutionary and belligerent dynamism...[28]

And now compare it with the following lines from *Dynamic and Synoptic Declamation* (also 1916):

I offered politicians the only solution to their financial problem: a gradual, canny sale of our artistic patrimony in order to multiply a hundredfold Italy's military, industrial, commercial and agricultural power, and to smash Austria forever, our eternally hated enemy.[29]

It would be erroneous to assume that an adequate image of Futurism could be inferred from an analysis of the manifestos alone, yet any definition of the movement not predicated upon a proper knowledge of their rhetorical structure would be seriously flawed. The Futurist manifesto is a set of imperatives as well as a literary performance; it constitutes indeed a new genre of literature.

Some of the manifestos are signed exclusively by Marinetti, others jointly by him and the painters Boccioni, Carrà, and Russolo (see, for instance, their

Against Passéist Venice which begins: "Venetians, when we shouted, 'let's murder the moonshine,' we were thinking of you, old Venice soiled with Romanticism!").

The presence of these painters, and in particular that of Boccioni, cannot be underestimated. It is Boccioni who, in 1910, authors the first technical manifesto of the entire movement, *The Technical Manifesto of Futurist Painters*. Two years later Marinetti brings out *The Technical Manifesto of Futurist Literature*, followed in 1913 by *The Destruction of Syntax, Wireless Imagination, Words in Freedom* and in 1914 by *Geometric and Mechanical Splendor and Numerical Sensibility*.[30]

Lexical and grammatical prescriptions resonate throughout these manifestos as well as a variety of recipes for an ideal Futurist text:

> Every noun must have its double, that is, the noun should be followed, with no conjunction, by the noun to which it is related by analogy. Example: man-torpedo-boat, woman-gulf, crowd-surf, piazza-funnel, door-faucet.
>
> Just as aerial velocity has multiplied our knowledge of the world, the perception of analogy becomes ever more natural to man. One must suppress the *like*, the *as*, the *so*, the *similar to*. Still better, one should deliberately confound the object with the image it evokes, foreshortening the image to a single essential word.[31]

Metalinguistic reflections are also not infrequent:

Except for needed contrasts or a change of rhythm, the different moods and tenses of the verb should be abolished, because they turn the verb into a stagecoach wheel, capable of adapting itself to rough country roads, but unable to turn swiftly on a smooth road. *The infinitive verb*, on the other hand, *is the very movement of the new lyricism,* having the fluency of a train's wheel or an airplane's propeller.[32]

Once velocity is assumed as both the principle governing the production of Futurist texts and the agent that actually gives them a shape, linear syntax and inherited forms of subordination cease to cohere adequately. Writing, for one, can no longer be fettered by referential obligations nor by unfulfilled desires of signification. It demands, instead, to be organized in a semiotic ritual where the incessant origin of meaning can be conjured up at any given point in time. Such a ritual was modelled on *simultaneity*, a direct outcome, if not a concomitant act, of velocity.

The faster space is traversed, the faster the distance between objects is reduced: ultimately it becomes inconsequential and the world returns to being flat like a painting.[33] Futurists tested this axiom with much exhuberance, especially in the early years of their progress. Boccioni claimed that *simultaneity* was the most signal contribution of the new school. In his *Pittura e scultura futurista* he stated:

> Simultaneity is the condition under which the different elements constituting dynamism reveal themselves...It is the result of that great cause which we call dynamism. It is the lyrical exponent of present conception of life, which is based on the rapidity and contemporaneity of knowledge and communication...[34]

When applied to written language, this means abandoning all hypotactic constructs. Propositions are abandoned in favor of verbal organizations where meaning (once limited to the exclusive domain of semantics) is determined by a variety of factors—from parataxis to graphemes, from typography and design to the adoption of non-canonical forms of punctuation.

All of this, naturally, makes new demands on the reader who is literally placed at the center of the text, just as the viewer had to be placed, in Boccioni's words, "at the center of the painting."[35] The destruction of distance and perspectivism brought about by ever increasing forms of velocity thus corresponds to a destruction of syntax, and it forces the reader/viewer to act both as a component of the work of art and as its necessary catalyst.

Predicated, as it is, on an index of acceleration, *simultaneity* bespeaks a situation in which all the symbols of any communicational sequence or cluster have the same opportunity to be conveyed. The Futurists, who were among the first avant-garde artists to see no obligatory connection between communication and information, did not construe this form of entropy as a negative condition. They regarded it as a truly democratic emancipation not only of lexicon, but of all actual and potential signifiers (linguistic and otherwise).[36]

In summation: as a language catalyst, man attaches signs to referents and ascertains a meaning that passes through them. This warrants his freedom to experience simultaneously the priority that creates them and the posteriority that consumes them; as an intrinsic component of his own work, he extracts from velocity the promise that his temporal dimension can be made to coincide with the ever-exceeding dimension of the work of art: an unsuppressable delirium of immortality.

Free-word compositions,[37] theatre syntheses and mixed media events, happenings *avant la lettre*, musical scores where the traditional distinction sound/noise is abolished—these are some of the genres that epitomize the most exciting segment of the Futurist offertory.

Free-wordism, according to Marinetti, is an attempt to capture the essential analogism that lies at the core of our being.[38] The notion of analogy upon which this statement is predicated categorically dispenses with all forms of comparisons. Far from serving as a factor of semantic amplification (or restraint) of its antecedent, each word is invited to establish its own metonymic chain reaction. Marinetti called analogy the "deep love" through which "distant, seemingly diverse and hostile things" find their points of contact.[39]

The expectations introduced by Futurist analogy could never have surfaced in Mallarmé's prose where analogy is featured as some sort of mysterious premonition leading to an object.[40] Furthermore, Futurism injects analogy with a method of madness and paves the way for a loss of referential and epistemological assertiveness. Literary texts must accept this loss in order to call into being historically acceptable processes of signification and hermeneutics.

To readers reluctant to assess text as an opportunity for discourse first and foremost, the idea of renouncing assertiveness may seem hardly Futuristic at all. The Futurists' well known predilection for the themes of war, velocity, aeronautics etc. would appear to be not only overwhelming, but also carefully chosen (and strictly observed) on account of their predetermined ideology. The argument here, however, is as follows: if the implications of Marinetti's "grammatical" manifestos are brought to their extreme and richest consequences, the analogical energy of any given semantic unit automatically fills the *horror vacui* that circumscribes that unit as soon as it is cast into a text. In the vortex of free-wordism, words and even alphabets recoil into primeval pictographic temptations, and the general tenor is such that writer and reader alike are constantly brought back to the ominous threshold that separates obscurity from light, oracularity from communication, and, more plainly, voice from language.

It is a threshold of which we find terrifying evidence in Paul's first letter to the Corinthians.[41] The apostle observes that obscure, poetic, analogic language (*o lalon glosse*) may indeed be used for praying. He who wishes to address people, however, must resort, or rather aspire, to *prophecy*, a term that signifies not so much an oracular utterance, but a form of linguistic competence aimed at explicating text.[42] Inspired as they may be by the Holy Spirit, prophecies are nonetheless dependent on sets of encoded expressions that prevent the speaker from sounding like a Barbarian, one for whom a language is nothing more than a medley of sounds. While the preference accorded to *prophecy* over *glosse* may be understandable (Paul's primary task is the edification of the Church), the feared association of Barbarians (and children) with linguistic acts that resist codification cannot help but leave a mark of disappointment in the heart of the would-be poet.

Yet this oscillation of language between sounds desiring to be words and words tempted to visit the sound cradle of their musical matrix has elicited positive responses as well.

In our own century, Gertrude Stein—ignorant as she may have been of Futurist theory and practice[43]—managed to construct writing in a fashion that would seem unthinkable without this a-referential notion of sign.

her *Poetry and Grammar*,[44] she maintains that Shakespeare could create a forest without ever mentioning any of the elements that make up a forest. This is like saying that meaning inferred from structures can, and, in fact, does replace meaning resulting from preconceived formulations of thought.

In this perspective genuine Futurist writing should not be defined by the notorious thematic obsessions of its practitioners. Indeed the given topic plays a totally inessential role and, just like the forest in Shakespeare, must be inferred from the text above and beyond the presence of referential terminology.

If we now look at Futurism as an idiom that has transcended its original confines and has instigated a large portion of contemporary thought, its revisitation should not require any form of genuflection. Profanation might be a more desirable approach. For a Futurist legacy to be meaningful, in fact, it is necessary that it be looted and ignored at the same time, made to signify above and beyond its premises. Marinetti himself is rather explicit about this in the final lines of *The Founding Manifesto*:

> Our fine deceitful intelligence tells us that we are the sum and the extension of our ancestors.—Perhaps!…So be it!…But who cares? We don't want to understand!…
>
> Woe to anyone who says those infamous words to us again!…[45]

Unfortunately, the first to disregard this exhortation was Marinetti himself, when he chose to be recognized as a legislating forefather rather than be assimilated as a Barbarian lost in the crowd. While Dada artists were beginning to metabolize Futurist proteins in post-war Europe, in Italy the Futurists began to play games with their own faith in simultaneity and became increasingly obsessed with politics. And where faith lived on, simple and pure, the courage to profess it faltered.

In 1919 Marinetti published *Les Mots en Liberté Futuristes*,[46] a collection of free-word manifestos, illustrated by the most noteworthy examples of his visual poems. It was perhaps a last ditch attempt to reclaim his most revolutionary innovations. 1919 is indeed a dramatically important year for the movement. Heated discussions on Futurist aesthetics persist in many circles, but the realization of Marinetti's most radical intuitions falls sadly by the wayside. The wonderful recapitulation of *Les Mots en Liberté Futuristes* is either neglected or forced to perform like a wild animal at the circus: it is no longer the transparent shell of the *will to power*, but the degraded testimony of a *will to act*.

What remains unaltered throughout all this travail is the Futurists' desire to define a post-humanistic culture. Scattered over hundreds of passages, the exaltation of the modern gadget is accompanied by the "barbaric" identification of man with mechanized nature.

The anthropocentric adventure that epitomizes the past is depicted as either dead or dying, and is pitched against an all-encompassing technological world. From the start, this *motif* had found particular favor in Marinetti's eyes:

> Sometimes the great human collectivities, howling tides of faces and arms, can make us feel a slight emotion. To them we prefer the great solidarity of motors, arrayed and eager.[47]

Motors, which were previously conceived as inanimate matter, are now accorded—through the use of a peculiarly revived *ornatus difficilis*[48]—the privilege of being breathing entities. In parallel, the emotional content offered by the sight of "great human collectivities" is drastically reduced.

No longer appreciated as a powerful opportunity to extend the sensorial and intellectual potential of humans, the machine begins to be seen as an ultimate goal in their evolution. This is the modernity of which Marinetti dreams, and he does so without any sense of loss. Man, who has been multiplied by the velocity of the speeding automobile, can now give up his role as the "maker of meaning." He prefers to be subsumed in the "molecular life" of the universe: his aesthetic task will be that of recording not his private lyrical obsession with matter, but the "lyric obsession of matter" itself.

This subsumption signals the artistic solution of the century-old difficulty encountered by man upon his confronting the industrialized world. The widespread concept of alienation, brought about by the reproductive machine, is here turned inside-out by the exhaltation of the modern gadget.

As late as 1921, amidst Futurist hesitations and Fascist manoeuvering, Antonio Gramsci could still write:

> They [the Futurists] have had the clear and precise notion that our time, the time of industrialization, of the big proletarian cities...needed new forms in art, in philosophy, in customs and in language: they did have this notion, which is clearly revolutionary, strictly Marxist.[49]

But even Gramsci could not sustain his enthusiasm for very long. In a letter to Trotsky, dated September 8, 1922, he recanted his endorsement:

> After the conclusion of the war, the futurist movement has lost all its characteristics...Those young intellectuals were rather reactionary. The workers who had seen in Futurism the elements of a struggle against the old stifling forms of Italian culture, so completely separated from the people, are now compelled again to fight for their freedom with real weapons, and have hardly any interest left for stalemate discussions.[50]

In view of the broken promises and contradictions for which Marinetti and the Futurists are responsible, Gramsci's sense of disorientation is indeed comprehensible. His "proletarian" approach, however, does not do justice to the subliminal drive that led them to deny the incontestable evidence of their capitulation. In this perspective the brief and enigmatic voice of the *diaphorìa* that filters through the pages of *The Untameables* had no real chance to be heard.

*

Under the rubric "Untameables," Marinetti has gathered a motley crew of criminals and perverts—vicious men chained to one another like filthy beasts. They live at the bottom of a pit, somewhere on a desert island, guarded by African soldiers who toss them chunks of the raw meat they butcher on the spot at feeding time. The soldiers, whose mastiff-like heads are kept locked in muzzles, blindly obey the Paper People—a race of beings shaped like cones surmounted by circumflex book-hats. The Paper People rule this forsaken island on behalf of their king, emperor, and god: His Majesty, Contradictor.

The grim living conditions of the Untameables may very well be based on the experience of World War I. Marinetti and many other eloquent advocates of war—Futurists and non-Futurists alike—fought on the Austrian-Italian front[51] and must have had ample opportunities to "admire" the spectacle of stinking, blood-filled trenches: a half-literal, half-metaphorical description of life at the front may be read between the lines in such passages as the following:

> [The Untameables'] legbands, frontlets and shiny steel collars had studs decorated with shreds of bloody flesh. Human flesh that was passed from man to man in their incessant squabbles. About twenty of these men-beasts had risen to their feet. Laboriously. Overcoming the weight of the chains welded to their wrists that held the herd of Untameables together. The trampled and whining weak ones writhed between the legs of the strong. Almost all of them were the color of coagulated blood and they were covered with great open sores, on their sides, their buttocks, their arms and their cheeks.[52]

In other passages a genuine Futuristic style is activated to render the madness and the internecine strife that characterize the life of the Untameables in the pit. Here and there emerge free-word juxtapositions that transcend the otherwise predictable and frequently unpunctuated list of adjectives and verbs:

> The weight of the chains and studded collars gave the fight a terrific rhythm, since the slowness of movement contradicted the furious speed of their eyes. Fists-pistons. Chests-bellows. Bodies-bottles grabbed around the neck by drunken hands.

—I've got you, you filthy dog!

—Why are you opening your mouth like that?

And down his throat, the fist. But the teeth bite down, and the fist comes out like a sponge drenched with blood. Two giant human pliers opened against one another. To pull out the invisible nail of the soul![53]

It is the kind of atrocity-inspired excitment that would eventually find its greatest protestation in Picasso's *Guernica*.

Every night the Untameables are released from the pit by order of the Paper People. Both the guards and prisoners cross a surreal oasis, at the center of which lies a lake of poetry and goodness.

Motionless and resplendent, a velvety splendor somewhere between white and blue, with infinite smiles of innocent children swimming in the silver water. No one was swimming in that motionless water; but its surface rippled now and then with fleeting apparitions. Gentle profiles of evanescent women, curves of exquisite nude bodies, misty locks of hair, fingers adorned with rings...

There was nothing in that lake, nothing. But all dreams bubbled sweetly there among velvets crystals and melodious jewels.[54]

Swimming and cavorting in the lake brings about a spiritual and physical metamorphosis. As they progress, parts of the Untameables' bodies begin to light up (the Paper People are fully lit). Prisoners and guards now "succumb" to brotherly love and happily saunter down to a most wondrous city:

> ...the first incandescent houses appeared. They were puzzling, fluid, built with unknown materials....
>
> Those fluid buildings were made out of a powerful vapor that flowed incessantly upward creating the walls, changing the mass, the volume, the protrusions and the architectural form, so that in time they could take the shape of a cube, a sphere, an egg, a pyramid and an upside-down cone. The buildings had no windows, but movable cracks, wounds, mouths, eyes, funnels that opened and closed according to the ever-changing whims and will of the inhabitants.[55]

Here the Untameables discover that the Paper People's supremacy is entirely dependent on the hard labor performed by paper mill workers. These workers' bodies have been partially atrophied by overly special-ized, assembly-line work. They demand that their abominable tasks be replaced with varied and person-alized jobs. They are so debilitated, however, that they cannot possibly mount an uprising against the Paper People. But the River People, who also work in the city, seem perfectly able to do so. In the words of a Paper Person who has embraced their cause:

...the River People are no longer the scattered, rejected and irresponsible people they once were. They've united to form a single river, and as such they no longer want to subject themselves to the embankments where they laboriously turn the great wheels of the illuminating motors. They want their river to flow freely through the Oasis, and to mix with the waters of the great Lake of Poetry, for therein lies the peace that they have demanded for so many years.[56]

The Untameables are overwhelmed by the desire to aid the revolutionaries. Mirmofim, their most loquacious and domineering spokesman,[57] succeeds in uniting revolutionary Paper People, River People, and the now-friendly guards.[58] Together they break down the cardboard dam that prevented the river from flowing into the Lake of Poetry.

Suddenly, after this furious and desperately hurried chain of events, the city is flooded and the Untameables run for their lives. The farther they get from the city, the more difficult their flight becomes: their bodies' luminosity decreases, only to be completely extinguished; the formerly friendly vegetation in the Oasis turns to metal and forces them out...The Untameables find themselves lying on the hot desert sand from which they had departed the night before.

At this point a new cycle of violence and death seems to resume. Mazzapà, the leader of the guards, dies, strangled by his chief prisoner. The Untameables are once again chained to one another and returned to their pit where the memory of their adventure is lost. Soon after some Paper People perform a concluding ritual:

> Like obedient mastiffs, the Negro soldiers offered their weary spherical heads to the Paper People, who methodically and unhurriedly clamped new muzzles on them. The locks could be heard creaking shut over their pug-nosed faces.[59]

The closing of the narrative circle might be expected to signal the end of the book. This, however, is not the case. In the last page of *The Untameables*—indeed, in the last two lines—Marinetti offers a *clavis lecturae* that throws a totally unexpected light on the entire novel: "the superhuman fresh-winged Distraction of Art, stronger than the raw dissonance of Sun and Blood, finally effected the metamorphosis of the Untameables."[60]

After much agitation and turmoil, a reflective disposition takes ahold of the Untameables. Once caught in an endless and mindless whirlpool of brutality, these characters now emerge from a long lethargy, and they are ready to recognize their desire for curiosity—not an instrument of experience, but an experience in and of itself. This new hunger interrupts the cycle of repeated events and extols the transcendental values of descent and resurrection.

The Oasis, the sweetness of its vegetation, the phosphorescence of its paths—these recollections begin to flash through Mirmofim's mind, and he painfully tries to fashion them into a fictional event. His former comrades and fellow protagonists are now his audience ("They all stood up and there was a commotion.—What do you see? Tell us! Tell us! Tell us what you see!"[61]), and he himself usurps the role of the author. This proposal of a narration within the narration is but the incipient phase of an unending game where awareness eclipses its own referents.

The "rules" of the game are laid out in Marinetti's concluding remarks where he introduces a provocative cause-and-effect relation between *memory* and *distraction*, two concepts normally perceived as contradictory. *Distraction*, furthermore, sets the stage for an uncanny and conspicuous paronomasia with *destruction*, a key word in the Futurist lexicon.

If memory, as Marinetti claims, brings about distraction (i.e. the removal of thought from objective reality), then the outcome of art predicated upon distraction connects thought to an artistic experience that must take place outside of objective reality itself. Distraction, in other words, implies a separate world of knowledge—a sensorial, shifting world that cannot be packaged in paradigms and handed down to future generations. While this world is not a replacement for the "inadequate world" that the Futurists had originally wanted to destroy, it is a world unfettered by the finality of construction. The meaning of "destruction" is no longer limited to "demolition"; it is revitalized as an action that principally opposes construction (*de-struere*). Distraction and destruction can thus be engaged in a metonymic binomial where the latter member incites the former. As it ceases to relate to decomposition and the liberation of space, destruction, as well as distraction, begins to focus on movement. The binomial operates, in fact, as a contiguity of incentives in the defunctionalizing of patterns: it is a difference in the making.

Two years after *The Untameables*, André Breton wrote:

> Language has been given to man so that he may make Surrealist use of it. To the extent that he is required to make himself understood, he manages more or less to express himself, and by so doing to fulfill certain functions culled from among the most vulgar...Not only does this unrestricted language, which I am trying to render forever valid, which seems to me to adapt itself to all of life's circumstances, not only does this language not deprive me of any of my means, on the contrary it lends me an extraordinary lucidity...I shall even go as far as to say that it instructs me and, indeed, I have had occasion to use *surreally* words whose meaning I have forgotten. I was subsequently able to verify that the way in which I had used them corresponded perfectly with their definition.[62]

The temptation to discover specimens of this linguistic confidence in Marinetti's prose is perhaps too enticing to neglect. Yet these specimens, if found, must be considered with great humility. There is at least one good reason why Futurism and Surrealism should be kept each in its own garden: their radically different approaches to oneiric work led them to endorse diametrically opposed political views. Indeed it would be embarrassing to parade Marinetti as a proto-Surrealist.[63]

In *The Untameables*, however, a relentless mixing of rhetorical registers invites a broadening, and a deepening, of the textual values that have all-too-frequently drawn and quartered Futurism. Marinetti does not wish to temper the harsh tones of tragic wine with comic water, as Elizabethan dramatists often did. He revels in the creation of uncalled-for proximities. Not unlike the Futurist painters who juxtapose green and purple—colors regarded as clashing at the time—Marinetti violently (and humorously) un-balances his prose.[64] Let us probe this assertion in the following examples. From his first appearance, Mirmofim, the surgeon, epitomizes gratuitous cruelty. Just before the Untameables reach the Oasis (the beauty of which leaves them all speechless), Mirmofim interrupts his account of how he amputated a leg that did not need to be amputated, only to intone a most morbid, pseudo-symbolistic song about a young lady who is being ferried away by Death itself:

Sister, sister
what a perfect
melancholy night!
Yet our mother was in tears
when she saw
that on the boat
death was sitting oh so near...[65]

A few pages later, inspired by the music of the Oasis, Mirmofim breaks into song once again, and this time:

The Untameables wanted to sing too. They tried to harmonize, but their harsh voices were broken by sobs shrieks raucous outbursts and comic wrong notes. The result was an atrocious cacophony.

—Keep quiet! shouted Mirmofim.—Let me sing alone. You're all off key.[66]

Preposterous is perhaps the epithet that most accurately describes Marinetti's willful avoidance of palatable transitions: in both meaning and sense he runs like a bandit. Heroic pledges, for instance, are frequently followed by descriptions of childish behavior; the most reactionary observations are grafted on desperately revolutionary deeds. Everything is pushed to the limit of credibility, and beyond.[67]

Just as the River People are about to raid the Dam,

the narrative tension is interrupted by the verbal quibblings of Notnor, Yessir, and Whoknows, three highly respected Paper People Governors who, each in his own way, try to stall and derail the revolutionary impetus of their subjects. Notnor's dialogue with Mirmofim offers a salacious example of Marinetti's sense of humor, spiked with an acerbic lyrical twist:

> In the pause of total silence, Notnor spoke:
>
> —Nooo! Nooo! Noooo! The River People will continue to obey!…They are brute force, quantity. Only we can command; we: who are quality!
>
> —That's untrue! shouted Mirmofim. Everything that used to be is wrong, because it used to be. Everything that has not been is right, because it has not been! It will be! Quality has been! We're going to do away with it! Quantity has never ruled! It shall rule! We will it!
>
> This sibylline speech agitated the crowd of revolutionary Paper People and semi-luminous men at the embankment. Even the River People didn't understand. Confusion, uneasiness.
>
> Wavering. Yes. No. Why? Is it me or him, the idiot? Murmuring of a skeptical sea. A rain of doubt on men's souls.[68]

Although no one has claimed that Marinetti should be assigned a place in any avant-garde movement other than Futurism, *The Untameables* is an essential and, in many respects, anticipatory document of the broad avant-garde discourse that gave significance to Euro-

pean culture *entre deux guerres*. Its stylistic noncha-
lance and deliberately devised insolvency of ordinary
logic point in a direction utterly divergent from the ob-
sequious indications of a critic like F.R. Flint. In a note
appended to the first American edition of the novel, he
describes *The Untameables* as a "stylistic compromise
between the radical free-wordism of *Zang Tumb Tumb*
(1914) which was primarily a performance libretto with
expensive typographical frills, and the normal florid art-
prose of the prewar years."[69]

The idea of calling Marinetti's innovations in visual
poetry "typographical frills" is at best ludicrous and
can be dismissed without any hesitation. As to the description of the book as "normal florid art-prose of the
pre-war years," it is nothing more than a perfunctory
elaboration of De Maria's already myopic assessment
of *The Untameables* as a "traditionally structured narrative."[70]

These clarifications *per se* may seem to be of little
interest, but they must be considered before a new perspective can be formulated: a sound stylistic and rhetorical analysis of *The Untameables* would discourage
anyone from even mentioning such terms as art-prose,
a rather vague expression often used to connotate a type
of writing concerned exclusively with the flowery effects of *belles lettres*. Although these "special" effects
are perceptible, here and there, in Marinetti's prose,
they do not at all represent the substance of his experi-
ment.

What matters in *The Untameables* is that paragraphs that could comfortably fit in a play by Beckett can co-exist with slapstick comedy right out of Abbott and Costello:

> His companion shook himself; then slowly began to get up as if he were bearing the whole burden of the heavy noon on his back. A little way off, there was a well. Dry, of course. Farther to the right, a pile of rocks. Vokur kneeled and with great effort lifted a sandy trapdoor. He took out two yellow bowls, filled with a muddy liquid....
>
> ...Vokur, sitting in the sand with his legs crossed, counted his breaths on his fingers, moving his torso back and forth so as not to lose count, and he watched the two bowls as they baked in the sun...[71]

Elsewhere the reader can walk through what might have been Fritz Lang's *Metropolis* had Alberto Savinio not remodelled it:

> Ambitious long-haired chimney peoples. Five Niagaras of fire. Staged naval battles. Daring leaps of gangways high over battleships shipwrecked in seas of mist. Outstretched fists of cranes fending off the assaults of rabid flames. Up high, the merry wheeling to and fro of tightrope dollies out of a circus. Rouge reflections on the fat cheeks of rivers. Broken evaporations shafts pimples of volcanos. Blasts from furnaces. Sledgehammers pounding. Sparklers. Ray-needles injecting fire into the dusky flesh of sick shadows. Air vents

panting like athletic trainers. Iron cages that detain
monkeylike fires with red-violet asses.[72]

The Untameables may not be the perfect example of
radical Futurism. It belongs nonetheless in that highly
experimental tradition that surfaced in Italy during the
second half of the nineteenth century with the so-called
Scapigliatura lombarda and writers like Vittorio
Imbriani.[73]

This tradition has reached the shores of contemporary literary consciousness with the writings of such
prose innovators as Gadda, Delfini and Landolfi. They
never failed to recognize that the primary responsibil-
ity of a writer resides in his ability to renew the language and the structure of the art he practices.

Had Marinetti continued to work in this direction
(instead of "Fascistizing" his prose), and had he used
his propagandistic genius to galvanize this textual ideology, the Moravias, Silones and Lampedusas would
have been revealed for the John Grishams, Michael
Crichtons, and Danielle Steels that they are, and modern Italian literature would have been spared the humiliation of seeing such mediocrity acclaimed as its
most significant representatives in the international
arena. It would have been a better "Italy at Vittorio
Veneto" for all of us.

Luigi Ballerini
Los Angeles, February 1994

NOTES

1. "e questo è il Nilo / che mi ha visto / nascere e crescere / e ardere d'inconsapevolezza" ("…this is the Nile / that saw me / come into the world and grow / and burn with unawareness"). "I Fiumi", 55–58, in *L'Allegria*, edited by Cristiana Maggi Romano, Milano, Mondadori, 1982, p. 143.

2. Marinetti, F.T. *Teoria e invenzione futurista*, edited by Luciano De Maria, Milano, Mondadori, 1968, pp. 963–97.

3. *ibid*. p. 988.

4. "Waiting for the Barbarians," in *Collected Poems*, translated by Edmund Keeley and Philip Sherrard, Princeton, Princeton University Press, 1992, pp. 18–19.

5. The verb "to wait" comes from the Old High German *wahten* which in turn comes from *wahta* (a guard, a watch). This etymology does not help us identify the sense of internal commotion and spiritual activity the verb is supposed to express here. These senses, on the other hand, are easily perceivable in the verb's Latinate equivalent, "to attend," which is derived from *ad-tendere* (to stretch toward) and subsumes the implications of both "to wait" and "to expect." The verb's root is also present in such lexemes as *tension, intention, intending* etc. In this essay the naked form of the Anglo-Saxon verb has been clad with Latin garments in an attempt to capture a special notion of towardliness, a notion implying tension and not necessarily movement. It is the kind of tension and alertness Paul desires for his fellow-Christians who are waiting for the Messiah: "As regards dates and times, brothers, there is no need for me to write to you, for you yourselves know perfectly well that the Day of the Lord will come like a thief in the night." (Paul of Tarsus, "Letter to the Community at Thessalonica" (1), 5.1, in *The Original New Testament*, edited and translated by Hugh J. Schonfield, London, Firethorn Press, 1985, pp. 280–81).

6 *Gli Indomabili*, Edizioni futuriste di "Poesia", Società Tipografica Editrice Porta, Piacenza, 1922.

7 Marinetti himself had a hard time defining it. "Adventure novel? symbolic poem? fantasy novel? fable? philosophical-social vision? None of these categories fit. It's a free-word book…" (Present edition, p. 63.) The issue of free-wordism and its legitimate application to *The Untameables* is discussed below. Marinetti's concern with the classification of his own work surfaces more than once in his writings. See, for instance, his introduction to *Mafarka le futuriste: roman africain* (Paris, E. Sansot, 1909), the first sentence of which reads as follows: "Here is the great flame-throwing novel I promised you. Just like our soul, it is polyphonic. It is at once a lyrical song, an epic poem, an adventure novel and a drama."

8 On March 23, 1919, at a meeting held in Milan at the Circolo dell'Alleanza Industriale e Commerciale of Piazza San Sepolcro (the birthplace of Fascism), Mussolini accused the Socialists of being a "clearly reactionary and wholly conservative party." His concluding remarks ("We decidedly oppose all forms of dictatorship, from the sword to the three cornered hat, from money to numbers; the only one we recognize is the dictatorship of will-power and intelligence.") must have sounded Futuristic enough to make Marinetti accept the nomination to the central committee of the *Fasci di combattimento* (these so-called "Fighting Leagues" were activist groups that formed the basic structure of incipient Fascism). For a full description of the genesis of the *Fasci*, see Renzo De Felice, *Mussolini il rivoluzionario*, Torino, Einaudi, 1965, pp. 501–523.

9 Marinetti and Mussolini's divergent points of view began to surface at the first Fascist Convention held in Florence on October 9, 1919. Mussolini delivered a rather bland and intentionally ambiguous speech which left hardly any time for other speakers. Marinetti's statement, on the other hand, was precise and to the

48

point. He championed, among other things, the necessity of "demanding, wanting, enforcing, the expulsion of the papacy, or...to use a more precise expression, the de-Vaticanization of Italy." After the electoral defeat of November 16, the Fascists held a new convention in Milan (May 24–25, 1920). Only ten—including Marinetti—of the original nineteen founding members were reappointed. It was unthinkable, however, that Marinetti could accept the accommodating platform proposed by Mussolini. The future Duce went as far as stating that "The Vatican represents 400 million men scattered the world over, and this enormous force ought to be exploited intelligently for the purpose of political expansion." (*Mussolini il rivoluzionario*, pp. 568–69 and 596–97). "On May 29, 1920," wrote the founder of Futurism, "Marinetti and some of the other Futurist leaders abandoned the Fighting Leagues because their anti-monarchic and anti-clerical stance had not been accepted by the majority of Fascists." (*Futurismo e fascismo*, in *Teoria e invenzione*, p. 442).

10 The Italian army's victory over the Austrians at Vittorio Veneto (November 4, 1918) brought about a rapid conclusion to World War I.

11 *Futurismo e fascismo*, in *Teoria e invenzione*, p. 430. This book, dedicated to his "dear and great friend, Benito Mussolini," is a transparent testimonial of Marinetti's unconditional surrender to Fascism. Marinetti's condemnation of Russian Futurism must seem ludicrous to anyone who is familiar with the Bolsheviks' art policy.

12 *ibid.*, p. 432 (italics mine). The discrepancy between Fascists and Futurists may be surmised from an amusing anecdote related by Gino Agnese in his biography of Marinetti: "As the November 16th elections approach, only in Milan are the Fascists able to produce a ticket...But the Milanese Fighting League, which is in better shape than any of the others, remains isolated. 'We must devise new forms of propaganda,' suggests Settimelli [an early

Futurist]…And he goes on: 'We need to spark people's curiosity. There's a circus in town, and that's just what we need. They'll lend us a crocodile and a leopard cub for a few hours: I propose that Mussolini and Marinetti parade themselves in the Galleria with these animals on a leash.' Mussolini cuts him off: 'Settimelli, don't be stupid!'" (*Marinetti: una vita esplosiva*, Roma, Camunia, 1990, pp. 219–220). True or not, it sure makes for a good story.

13 The popular name of the Fascists' "Italian Social Republic" (Sept. 1943 – April 1945). Many of its administrative offices were located at Salò, on the western shore of Lake Garda.

14 "Your Majesty, I bring to you *l'Italia di Vittorio Veneto*." It is commonly assumed that Mussolini pronounced this "historical phrase" on the occasion of his first meeting with the king (October 30), but we cannot be one hundred per cent sure. According to Antonino Répaci (*La marcia su Roma*, Milano, Rizzoli, 1972, p. 567) Mussolini spoke these words. To give credence to his assumption, Répaci invokes the authority of Giacomo Acerbo, "who was there." The latter, however, declares not to have heard any such utterance. "…I am almost positive that Mussolini did not say this when the king, surrounded by his generals, received him at court. He may have said it in the course of the private conversation he had with the king afterwards." (*Fra due plotoni di esecuzione*, Bologna, Cappelli 1968, p. 185). Be as it may, there is little doubt that in those days Mussolini was particularly fond of the symbolic values of the expression. On October 29, fearing perhaps that the king might order the army to stifle the barely finished March on Rome, Mussolini wrote: "The army…must not interfere. The Fascists confirm their highest admiration for the soldiers who fought at Vittorio Veneto. The Fascists are not marching against the police either; they are marching against a weak and downright stupid political class that has been incapable of providing the nation with a government for four long years." (*Il popolo d'Italia*, n. 259,

IX; now in *Opera Omnia di Benito Mussolini*, edited by Edoardo & Duilio Susmel, Florence, La Fenice, 1972, vol. XVIII, p. 462). On October 31 Mussolini wired Prime Ministers Andrew Bonard Law and Raymond Poincaré to alert them that his appointment was a reflection of the *"idealità italiane di Vittorio Veneto"* ("Italian ideals born at Vittorio Veneto"). Again, on November 2, a telegram sent by Mussolini to Piero Marsich, a former member of the Central Committee of the Fascist Party, reads as follows: "I have always known we would meet again. Brotherly thanks for your oath of allegiance, which I accept with great joy. *L'Italia di Vittorio Veneto* lives and shall live forever." (*Opera Omnia*, 1956, vol. XIX, pp. 377 & 380).

15 In a letter to Francesco Cangiullo, dated April 22 of the same year (F.T. Marinetti—F. Cangiullo, *Lettere*, edited by Ernestina Pellegrini, Firenze, Vallecchi, 1989, p. 140), Marinetti mentions a lecture he delivered on *The Untameables* at Il Cabaret del Diavolo, which opened in Rome on April 19, 1922, in the basement of the Hôtel Elite et des Etrangers. Thus the book must have been written at least a few months before the "March on Rome." Incidentally, Mussolini did not really "march." He arrived on October 30 by train (the "direttissimo" 17), which pulled in the station one and a half hour behind schedule.

16 Present edition, p. 66 (italics mine).

17 *ibid*, p. 73.

18 Although it was established in 1926, the official opening took place on Oct. 28, 1929 (the seventh anniversary of the March on Rome). Thirty of the sixty members were nominated by Mussolini and subsequently appointed by the King of Italy. Mussolini himself chose the remaining thirty members from names proposed by the Academicians. This clearly Fascist Academy was created to counter non-Fascist institutions at a time when intellectuals still enjoyed a certain amount of political freedom. Such freedom, how-

ever, would soon be curtailed by the obligatory oath of allegiance to the Fascist party.

19 Even at the time of its original appearance, the book was hailed as a masterpiece by very few reviewers, namely: Marinetti's wife, Benedetta ("Gli Indomabili di F.T. Marinetti," *L'Impero*, I, n. 54, May 13, 1923), Francesco Cangiullo ("Gl'indomabili: Lettera aperta di Cangiullo a Marinetti," *Piccolo Giornale d'Italia*, August 18, 1922), R. G. ("Gli 'Indomabili' di Marinetti," *Giornale della Sera*, Napoli, September 30, 1922), Mario Hyerace ("Gli Indomabili di F.T. Marinetti," no bibliographical data available at present; the text may be found in the Futurist Collection of the Getty Center for the History of Art and the Humanities). To this we must add an anonymous handwritten "report" advising a French publisher (Sansot?) against printing a translation of Marinetti's novel which is referred to as *La nuit des Indomptables* (also at the Getty Center). The only contemporary review that would seem to have any critical value is Silvio Benco's "Due libri africani su [di?] Marinetti" (*La Nazione*, Trieste, August 18, 1922). It has been translated in the appendix to the present edition. Marinetti's response, which was published in Bruno Sanzin's *Marinetti e il Futurismo* (Trieste, 1924, pp. 29–31), has been translated here as well.

20 See Gaetano Mariani's *Il primo Marinetti* (Firenze, Le Monnier, 1970), and in particular the pages dedicated to the *La conquête des étoiles*. Here, among other things, Mariani observes that *La conquête* "...written in 1902, could be called an aesthetic celebration of war cast in analogical forms..." and that in this poem dynamism and velocity, two fundamental concepts of Futurism, "are the two essential elements associating the portrayal of war with an emblem of Beauty." pp. 61–62. Marinetti indeed began his career as a French writer, and, as late as 1909, confessed to his friend Aldo Palazzeschi that he did not feel comfortable writ-

ing in Italian. See Palazzeschi's preface to *Teoria e invenzione*, p. X.

21 See F.T. Marinetti's *Let's Murder the Moonshine: Selected Writings*, Los Angeles, Sun & Moon Press, 1991, pp. 47–52. Quotations taken from this text have been altered, when necessary, for greater accuracy.

22 "1. We intend to sing the love of danger, the habit of energy and fearlessness. 2. Courage, audacity and revolt will be essential elements of our poetry." etc. (*Let's Murder the Moonshine*, p. 49).

23 E.R. Curtius has collected significant examples of this topos, ranging from from Dante's "L'acqua ch'io prendo già mai non si corse" (*Paradiso*, II, 7) to Ariosto's "Cosa non detta mai in prosa né in rima" (*Orlando Furioso* I, 2), and consequently to Milton's "Things unattempted yet in Prose or Rhime" (*Paradise Lost*, I, 16). *European Literature and the Latin Middle Ages*, Princeton, Princeton University Press, 1990, p. 86.

24 *Let's Murder the Moonshine*, p. 47.

25 *ibid.*, pp. 50–51.

26 The term was coined by Marinetti to stigmatize those people whose philosophy of art and life did not conform to Futurism. It defines, specifically, the modern pedant, the *laudator temporis acti*.

27 A person opposing Italy's intervention in World War I.

28 *Let's Murder the Moonshine*, p. 138.

29 *ibid.*, p. 150.

30 The normative characteristics of these manifestos seem to be primarily rooted in the example set by Boccioni.

31 "Technical Manifesto" in *Let's Murder the Moonshine*, pp. 92–93.

32 "Geometric and Mechanical Splendor," *ibid.*, p. 107.

33 Futurism seems to be claiming for itself the aesthetic privilege granted to painting (a two dimensional art based on light and shadow, capable of acquiring depth through perspective) over sculpture (a three dimensional art lacking real perspective) by

many Italian Renaissance artists and writers. See in particular Leonardo da Vinci who under the heading, "That sculpture is a lesser craft than painting, and lacks many characteristics of nature," wrote: "...In the first place sculpture requires a certain light, that is from above, a picture carries everywhere with it its own light and shade. Thus sculpture owes its importance to light and shade, and the sculptor is aided in this by the nature of the relief which is inherent in it, while the painter whose art expresses the accidental aspects of nature, places his effects in the spots where nature must necessarily produce them. The sculptor cannot diversify his work by the various natural colours of objects; painting is not defective in any particular. The sculptor when he uses perspective cannot make it in any way appear true; that of the painter can appear like a hundred miles beyond the picture itself. Their [the sculptors'] works have no aerial perspective whatever..." (*The Notebooks of Leonardo da Vinci*, compiled and edited by Jean Paul Richter, New York, Dover, 1970, vol. I, p. 329). See also the letter (dated Feb. 18th, 1546) that Iacopo da Pontormo sent to Benedetto Varchi in response to the latter's questionnaire on the comparison between painting and sculpture: "But what I called too daring is that importance placed on outdoing nature in wanting to give life to a figure, to make it seem alive and yet to place it on a flat surface, because if the painter had considered at all that when God created man he sculpted him in the round, which makes it easier to give life to a figure, then he would not have taken up a discipline so full of artifice, so miraculous and divine." See original text in *Trattati d'arte del Cinquecento*, edited by Paola Barocchi, Bari, Laterza, 1960, p. 68.

34 Milano, Edizioni futuriste di Poesia, 1914. Now in *Gli scritti editi e inediti*, edited by Zeno Birolli, Milano, Feltrinelli, 1971, p. 176. The notion of simultaneity, a cornerstone of the Futurist edifice, never ceased to attract the attention of Futurist theoreticians. As

late as 1937—sixteen years after Boccioni's death—Bruno Corra could still write: "Simultaneity—still today and forever—means analogy, images. The lyrical core that lies at the base of Marinetti's poem (what an ancient poet called a *canto*, and what Marinetti today calls a *simultaneity*) is in itself a great image that includes and conditions a hundred, a thousand others. Mixing, in a single act of creative imagination, the past and the future, that which is near and that which is far, the phosphorescent fermentation of psychological life and the fluid mass of sensorial perception— this means making analogical transformation the essential, intimate law of one's own art." See "Marinetti poeta delle parole in libertà simultanee," *Rassegna Nazionale*, January, 1938 (XVI). The essay had been written as a twenty page autonomous pamphlet to be published one year earlier by the Stabilimento Tipografico del Genio Civile, Roma. The galleys of this pamphlet may be found in the Futurist Collection of the Getty Center. The passage cited here is from page 14. The poem by Marinetti to which Corra makes reference is *Il Poema Africano della Divisione 28 Ottobre*. It is indeed divided into fifty-nine "simultaneous syntheses." A new synthesis, hitherto unpublished, has recently surfaced from the papers at the Getty Center.

35 *Gli scritti editi e inediti*, p. 173.

36 In this respect, Futurist writings ought to be analyzed as *de facto* anticipations of much contemporary theoretical work. Consider, for instance, the following excerpt from Jacques Derrida's *Of Grammatology*: "For some time now, as a matter of fact, here and there, by a gesture and for motives that are profoundly necessary, whose degradation is easier to denounce than it is to disclose their origin, one says 'language' for action, movement, thought, reflection, consciousness, unconsciousness, experience, affectivity, etc. Now we tend to say 'writing' for all that and more: to designate not only the physical gestures of literal pictographic or ideographic

inscriptions, but also the totality of what makes it possible; and also, beyond the signifying face, the signified face itself. And thus we say 'writing' for all that gives rise to an inscription in general, whether it is literal or not and even if what it distributes in space is alien to the order of the voice: cinematography, choreography, of course, but also, pictorial, musical, sculptural 'writing.' One might also speak of athletic writing, and with even greater certainty of military or political writing in view of the techniques that govern those domains today." (Baltimore, Johns Hopkins, 1976, p. 9)

37 Preceded as they were by words in freedom proper, actual free-word compositions—visually oriented, spatially organized poetic texts—begin to appear in 1914 and continue well into the Forties. The most comprehensive anthology of these visual writings is *Tavole parolibere futuriste (1912–1944)*, edited by Luciano Caruso and Stelio Maria Martini, Napoli, Liguori, 1975.

38 "...in order to express the exact value and the proportions of the life he has lived, a narrator blessed with the gift of lyricism will cast his nets far and wide. Thus he will telegraphically express the analogical foundation of life; in other words, he will achieve the same economic speed that the telegraph gives to the superficial tales of reporters and war correspondents. This need for laconism relates not only to the laws of speed by which we are governed, but also to the special rapport that poets have enjoyed with their audiences throughout the centuries." ("Destruction of Syntax Wireless Imagination Words in Freedom" in *Teoria e invenzione*, p. 61).

39 "Technical Manifesto" in *Let's Murder the Moonshine*, p. 93.

40 See for instance Stéphane Mallarmé's "Le Démon de l'analogie" in *Divagations* (first published in 1897), Geneva, Éditions d'art Albert Skira, 1943, pp. 21–23.

41 I, XIV, 1–25.

42 This meaning of the word *prophecy* is unique to New Testament Greek.

43 She did, however, write a *poème en prose* entitled "Marry Nettie." Although it is in no way a homage to Futurism, this farcical specimen of Steinean bravura acknowledges—if nothing else—Marinetti's notoriety: "...Marry who. Marry Nettie. Which Nettie. My Nettie. Marry whom. Marry Nettie. Marry my Nettie..." (*Painted Lace*, Yale University Press, New Haven, 1955, pp. 42–48).

44 See *Lectures in America*, Random House, New York, 1935.

45 *Let's Murder the Moonshine*, p. 52.

46 Milano, Edizioni futuriste di "Poesia", 1919.

47 "Geometric and Mechanical Splendor" in *Let's Murder the Moonshine*, p. 106.

48 Marinetti had in fact warned against its implementation: "Be careful not to force human feelings onto matter. Instead, divine its different governing impulses, its forces of compression, dilation, cohesion, and disaggregation, its crowds of massed molecules and whirling electrons. We are not interested in offering dramas of humanized matter. The solidity of a strip of steel interests us for itself; that is, the incomprehensible and non-human alliance of its molecules and its electrons that oppose, for instance, the penetration of a howitzer." ("Technical Manifesto of Futurist Literature" in *Let's Murder the Moonshine*, p. 95).

49 *L'Ordine Nuovo*, January 5, 1921. See *L'Ordine Nuovo*, Milano, Feltrinelli, 1966.

50 In response to a letter of inquiry Leon Trotsky had sent to the editors of *Literatura i revoljutsija*. Gramsci's letter was written in Moscow, and it is dated September 8, 1922. An Italian version of the text can be found in Antonio Gramsci's *Opere*, Torino, Einaudi, 1966, vol. XI, pp. 527–28.

51 For a boastful and quite enjoyable account of Marinetti's actions in World War 1, see his *L'alcova d'acciaio* (*The Steel Alcove*),

Milano, Mondadori, 1927. This book was re-issued in 1985 by Serra & Riva (with a delightful introduction by Alfredo Giuliani).

52 Present edition, p. 94

53 *ibid.*, p. 94–95

54 *ibid.*, p. 147

55 *ibid.*, p. 171–172

56 *ibid.*, pp. 184

57 Only a few characters are mentioned by name in *The Untameables*: Curguss, Kurotoplac, Kizmicà, Vokur, Mazzapà etc. See also translator's note.

58 Plus a group of incipient beings called the "Semi-Luminous."

59 Present edition, p. 215

60 *ibid.*, p. 218

61 *ibid.*, p. 217

62 *Manifestoes of Surrealism*, University of Michigan Press, Ann Arbor, 1972, pp. 32–34.

63 It would be impossible, however, to appreciate Breton's notion of analogy (the coming together of "two distant realities" capable of producing *the light of the image*—see *Manifestoes...*, pp. 36–37) without thinking of Marinetti's "deep love" connecting distant objects. On the other hand, the following *caveat* from the surrealist manifesto might be read as an implicit polemic against Futurism: "The principle of the association of ideas...militates against it [i.e. man's rational ability to effect the juxtaposition of distant realities]. Or else we would have to revert to an elliptical art, which Reverdy deplores as much as I." *ibid.*, p. 37.

64 In this respect *The Untameables* is not a totally unexpected event. In 1915, for instance, Bruno Corra had published *Sam Dunn è morto*, a most pleasant example of fiction in which plot, character development and all other attendant features of realistic prose are constantly disregarded in favor of lexical and analogical "acrobatics." This book was reprinted by Einaudi (Torino) in 1970. In

more recent times, John Lennon's *A Spaniard in the Works* (London, Jonathan Cape, 1965) bears witness—I believe—to the vitality of this experimental tradition.

65 Present edition, p. 116

66 *ibid.*, p. 130

67 And not just in this novel. Certain qualities of Marinetti's style remained constant throughout his career. In his later works, however (see, for instance, *Poema Africano della Divisione 28 Ottobre* or, better still, *Quarto d'ora di poesia della X Mas*, his very last poem), a sense of mechanical darkness replaces the mirthful anarchy of, let us say, *Mafarka il futurista*. Here the eponymous hero's coiled-up penis—11 yards long—is mistaken for an anchor cable and causes its owner to be dragged on the ocean for many a nautical mile. An Italian magistrate, whose intelligence was inversely proportionate to Mafarka's sexual endowment, prosecuted Marinetti on a charge of obscenity. The episode inspired Aldo Palazzeshi to make the following comment: "Had it been a question of skillfully dosed-out centimeters, that description could have seen as bordering on, or perhaps breaking the bounds of obscenity, but eleven yards...Your Honor!?" (*Teoria e invenzione*, XIV).

68 Present edition, p. 200–201

69 See F.T. Marinetti's *Selected Writings*, New York, Farrar, Strauss and Giroux, 1972, p. 246.

70 *Teoria e invenzione*, p. LXVIII. De Maria does, however, address the "allegorizing" value of the novel. Moreover, his recognition of Marinetti's failure to deliver a convincing free-word novel does not translate into a trivialization of free-wordism itself.

71 Present edition, pp. 79–80

72 *ibid.*, p. 173–174. Fritz Lang's film (1926) was first mentioned in connection with *The Untameables* by De Maria. His allusion, however, is made in all seriousness and refers to the scene where the River People riot (Present edition p. 205).

73 "A mid-19th century avant-garde moveme
enced by Baudelaire, the French Symbo
Poe, and German Romantic writers, it s
sical, Arcadian, and moralist traditio
works that featured bizarre and pathologica.
realistic, narrative description. One of the founu..
Cletto Arrighi (pseudonym for Carlo Righetti), coined the .
for the group, whose chief spokesmen were the novelists Giuseppe
Rovani and Emilio Praga." (*The New Encyclopedia Britannica,*
15th edition, Chicago, *Encyclopedia Britannica,* 1974, vol. 8, p.
945). Recently, critics have begun to re-evaluate the novellas of
Vittorio Imbriani (1840–1886), professor of aesthetics at the University of Naples, and they have recognized the modernity of his
resilient and somewhat bizarre style.

TRANSLATOR'S NOTE

The Untameables was first published as one of the Futurist editions of *Poesia* (Piacenza, Porta, 1922). The
present translation is based on Luciano De Maria's edition (*Teoria e invenzione futurista*, Milan, Mondadori,
1968). It was previously translated by Arthur A.
Coppotelli (Farrar, Straus and Giroux, 1972). Traces of
his translation may surface here and there in this version.

Meticulous care has been taken to reproduce
Marinetti's idiosyncratic punctuation. Many of
Marinetti's technical terms have been restored, such
as "tactilism" etc. Proper names have generally been
kept in the original, unless a specific meaning could
be detected in the Italian pronunciation. In these cases
they have either been translated, or their original meaning has been rendered in a footnote.

J.P.

THE FREE-WORD STYLE

How would one define *The Untameables*? Adventure novel? symbolic poem? fantasy novel? fable? philosophical-social vision? None of these categories fit. It's a free-word book. Nude raw synthesized. Simultaneous polychrome polyclamorous. Vast violent dynamic.

No doubt I had it in my free veins and my free muscles when as a naked baby I would play with the naked Negro urchins on the burning dunes of Ramleh. A brown Bedouin tent hemmed with scrawny dogs rags carrion garbage. Red silence of the Negroes' faces crouched around an aromatic fire. Crackling. Spiral of blue smoke. Absolute silence. The air an anxious crystal. The silence whines. A flute. Dreaming perhaps of squeezing out the sweetness of the purest of green evenings.

Undoubtedly I had *The Untameables* in my blood during my last trip to Upper Egypt. But the idea for this free-word poem struck me when I was dozing one morning in September, a few days after I had finished *l'Alcova di acciaio* [*The Steel Alcove*] at Antignano. Red banners fluttered over the factories in Livorno occupied by the workers. But they seemed gray against the scarlet white Negro laugh of the inspirational sea.

Words in freedom include momentous works.

After my first words in freedom: *Battaglia peso + odore* [*Battle Weight + Smell*] (August 11, 1912) and *Zang tumb tumb*, *Piedigrotta* by Francesco Cangiullo, *Ponti sull'oceano* [*Bridges over the Ocean*] by Luciano Folgore, *L'Ellisse e la spirale* [*The Ellipsis and the Spiral*] by Paolo Buzzi, *Guerrapittura* [*War-painting*] by Carrà, *Rarefazioni e parole in libertà* [*Rarefaction and Words in Freedom*] by Corrado Govoni, *Baionette* [*Bayonets*] by Auro d'Alba, *Archi Voltaici* [*Voltaic Arcs*] by Volt, *Equatore notturno* [*Nocturnal Equator*] by Francesco Meriano, *Firmamento* [*Firmament*] by Armando Mazza, and *Les mots en liberté futuristes* [*Futurist Words in Freedom*] by Marinetti have been circulated by the Futurist issues of *Poesia* throughout Italy and the entire world.

From other publishers and at exhibitions, there appeared free-word compositions by Balla, Boccioni, Buzzi, Cangiullo, Caprile, Carli, Carrozza, Cerati, Primo Conti, De Nardis, Depero, Folicaldi, Forti, Ginna, Guglielmino, Guizzidoro, Illari, Jamar 14, Jannelli, Leskovic, Mainardi, Marchesi, Masnata, Morpurgo, Nannetti, Nicastro, Olita, Pasqualino, Presenzini

Mattioli, Rognoni, Sandri Sandro, Settimelli, Simonetti, Ardengo Soffici, Soggetti, Soldi, Steiner.

Free-wordism has triumphed and influenced all literature around the world. Foreign avant-garde reviews are full of words in freedom.

Words in freedom orchestrate colors, noises, sounds, they mix the materials of languages and dialects, arithmetic and geometric formulas, musical notation, old, deformed or new words, the cries of animals, of wild beasts and motors.

Words in freedom split the history of thought and human poetry neatly in two, from Homer to the earth's last breath of lyricism.

Before us, men had always sung like Homer, with a narrative sequence and a logical catalog of events, images, ideas. There is no substantial difference between Homer's poetry and Gabriele D'Annunzio's.

Our free-word compositions, instead, finally distinguish us from Homer since they no longer contain narrative sequence, but rather the simultaneous polyexpression of the world.

Words in freedom are a new way of seeing the universe, an essential evaluation of the universe as the sum of forces in movement that intersect at the finish-line of our creative-ego's consciousness, and are simultaneously recorded with all the expressive means at our disposal.

A field of extremely difficult research full of uncertainties, far from success and public approval. Heroic attempts of the spirit projecting itself beyond all its norms of logic and convenience.

Our words in freedom give birth to the new synthesized Italian style, rapid, simultaneous, incisive, the new style completely freed from all the classical frills and robes, a style capable of wholly expressing the souls of the ultrarapid victors at Vittorio Veneto.

Destruction of the sentence with its steps, festoons, and drapery. Short sentences without a verb. Punctuation used only to avoid ambiguity. Words isolated between full-stops in order to create ambience or atmosphere.

I offer to the public and to future critics some typical samples of this new Italian style. I'll begin with a passage from *Crepapelle* [*Bursting Out of One's Skin*], a volume of grotesque short stories by Luciano Folgore, the powerful and revered free-word poet who also wrote *Ponti sull'Oceano* [*Bridges over the Ocean*]:

A small terrace to the west: an iron and slate footbridge for exploring that bit of sea painted on the doormat on the balcony in front.

We're on the top floor. A hundred twenty-nine steps. (The fat landlady weeps because of them and she counts them every day, and she eats my sunflower seeds while chitchatting with her bony neighbors sunken in their lettuce green bathrobes).

On my left foot I wear a tarnished brass chain attached to

the wood perch that never stops swinging ɛ
say yes even to the raucous crow, I try my h
ways at the world.

The world seen from a slant is a different thing. ᴗ
Grotesque. Turned a bit on itself. In a difficult position. Continuously in fear of losing its balance.

I'll take a passage from Cangiullo's *Roma sotto la pioggia* [*Rome in the Rain*], published in 1916 in *Piccolo Giornale d'Italia*:

And the station's there for the ones on leave: even the windscreen of its canopy is dripping...

A train of war veterans howls on arrival like a black hyena that's devoured an enemy camp.

Outside in the square an automobile flies by splashing.

A rain desert.

A desert of city squares sizzling with rain.

The obelisk of the 500, in Piazza del Popolo, the column in Piazza Colonna, upright, impassive petrified guards in the rain coming down in elevators.

And it's raining amid the botanical bodies of Villa Borghese and on the mineral nymphs of the Esedra fountain who have grown accustomed only to water...

Then

a *delivery girl* and a militarized *tram conductor*

without umbrellas

one

behind
the other
along the wall
like 2 human dogs.
Quarter to 11.

I'll take a passage, at random, from Angelo Rognoni's novel: *La veste che faceva frou-frou* [*The Dress That Went Frou-frou*]:

We went into an alley. Black, rot, damp, damp, mold, stubs, unhinged doors, windows askew, taverns, dogs lying down, stink of wine, oil, sinister faces of thugs, unbuttoned pants, gnarled cudgels, mora, mafia, clinking of coins, spoiled apples, rotten cabbage, snail slime, orange lights escaping from under doorways, from long hallways, from half-drawn shades: "slums".

We went into a low house, a red room, through a tangle of veils, of nudity, of mirrors, of flashes, of strong perfume, of cigarette smoke, of rouge, of powder.

I can easily demonstrate how Futurist words in freedom have not only triumphed in world literature, but have also influenced journalism.

In narrative and descriptive articles you can find passages of rapidified, synthesized, essential style, and at times real words in freedom with the relative leaps of thought, notation and simultaneity.

We quote at random from an article by Fraccaroli in *Corriere della Sera* entitled *Frontiers*:

> Alps, valleys, tunnels (close the windows, quick!), the Ticino River roaring, villages with their hooded houses, acute angle, very little snow on the highest peaks, a cool wind, Swiss trainmen speaking to you in Lombard-Ticinese, in German to your neighbor with his head shaved, in French to that lady sitting by herself.
>
> The train speeds along.
>
> . . . .
>
> Here is the Lake of the Four Cantons† A white steamboat, the sunset plucks the petals of violets over the lake, squirts red paint on the barren mountains, towns garlanded with flowers and inscriptions huddle on the shores; then at the farther end Lucerne dressing with fireflies. The train bloats with passengers: packed compartments, bursting corridors. At Lucerne, overflow of the crowd, up and down. The train remains full to the brim. Two hours later, Basel.

Balilla Pratella writes in *Popolo d'Italia*: "With their essentiality, words in freedom have now won over our greatest men and writers: including Gabriele D'Annunzio who, in his recent *Notturno* [*Nocturne*], ingeniously used them in the first 130 pages, and on page 124, for

---

† Lake Lucerne.

example, he has achieved effects similar to the famous
"*Flames flames flames…*" in F. T. Marinetti's *Battaglia
di Adrianopoli* [*Battle of Adrianople*].

Here is the passage that Pratella alludes to:

> Faces faces faces, all the passions of all the faces race
> across my wounded eye, numberless, like hot sand through
> clenched fingers. No one stops. But I recognize them.

Giuseppe Lipparini writes in *Resto del Carlino*:

> Do you remember Marinetti's words-in-freedom campaign
> against syntax? It was necessary to rid oneself of every rule,
> to free the oppressed word from the slavery in which the
> bonds of syntax were holding it, to kill the sentence, to de-
> compose the clause. It was necessary to suppress every idea
> of subordination, and to express oneself only through coor-
> dinates. And these coordinates were to be reduced to their
> essential terms in order to reduce them to isolated words
> and pure expression. Thus the word, a marvelous living crea-
> ture, would recover its splendor and be freed from the heavy
> veil of fog and tedium that veiled its luminous face.

.   .   .   .

> And there was even an advantage to this, because from
> it there came the taste for a more varied, more agile prose
> style, richer in surprises, more broken up, not in the French
> manner which was poorly used in earlier times, but in ac-
> cordance with an almost plastic concept of the collocation
> of words.

Now I open *Notturno*, Lipparini continues, and read pages like this:

The city is full of ghosts.
Men walk with no sound, wrapped in soot.
The canals smolder.
A drunkard singing, a shout, a spat.
Blue lights in the smoke.
The yell of the spotter planes made raucous by the mist.

Or even more significantly:

The motor launch for Sant'Andrea throbs at the landing.
I'm taking with me the luggage and the message pouch.
Rough lagoon.
Water splashes.
The Sicilian engineer with whom I'm chatting.

And again:

...We're leaving.
The San Marco basin, blue.
Sky everywhere.
Wonder, despair.
The motionless veil of tears.
Silence.
The pulse of the engine.
Here are the *Giardini*.
We turn into the canal.

And in *Notturno* I can also quote other typically free-word fragments:

Bandaged head.

Closed mouth.

The right eye injured, livid.

Right jaw broken: swelling begins.

Olive-skinned face: an unusually serene expression.

Upper lip sticks out a little, a bit swollen.

Cotton swabs in the nostrils.

Sultry flowers and wax.

The black pall, unchanged. The form of the corpse, unchanged.

Two sailors on guard.

The noises of the day from outside. The horns, the bells, the city waking up, the inevitable beginning again.

Blue water, felicity of golden air, flocks of seagulls laughing about their silly laugh.

Darkness. Wandering shadows. Chatter. Smell of cooking, shadows of poverty.

Grieving faces of Marys, faces strained from work and bad luck, pitiful faces.

Emaciated children, all eyes, filthy, sad.

The diseased water in the canal.

The reddish house with the ten funnel-shaped chimneys.

I turn around. I get off. War! War! Faces. Faces. Faces.

All the passions on all the faces. Ashes. It's a March rainstorm. Bora. Rain. I eavesdrop on the downpour.

The great free-wordist Paolo Buzzi, after having quoted this passage, says: "To its credit, the book is full of these zones of words in freedom. It's a truth that does not have to be shouted too loudly. All of Italy is saying it by now, and—of course—the whole world where our Futurism, of us post- and anti-D'Annunzians, is what it is: not just as of today, naturally."

At the opening of the great Casa d'Arte Bragaglia in Rome, I expressed my satisfaction with all this to Folgore, Cangiullo, Carli, Settimelli, Pannaggi, and with the young Futurist painters Fornari, Paladini, Scirocco, Verderame, Tato, Somenzi. The eloquent joy of our free-word spirits elastically intersected by the exciting lighted ceilings and dynamic walls created by Balla, Depero, Virgilio Macchi.

The great Futurist decorative art has been realized. In Rome, yes, in Rome, which could not continue to be the sole fortress of traditionalism. Rome is becoming more and more powerful as the capital of the new Italy of Vittorio Veneto; it is becoming and will become the power plant of world Futurism.

F. T. MARINETTI

THE UNTAMEABLES

1

THE DUNE OF CAMELS

—Vokur! Vokur! Wake up! I'm thirsty,—said Mazzapà, a herculean Negro dressed in white, seated, with his legs crossed, on the burning sand, intently cleaning his rifle which had clusters of blinding sparks on the barrel and the bayonet.

On the crest of the dune not another living thing could be seen, so it seemed the Negro was talking to the desert.

A long, glaring silence.

—Vokur! Wake up! I'm thirsty.

Another figure altered the silhouette of the dune: it was Vokur who shuddered and did not wake, lying there on his back, with his eyes half-closed. His mouth gaping. Like a corpse. Next to him, three other Negroes petrified by sleep and the murderous light. All of them wore, clumsily, uniforms of white colonial soldier canvas. Great nude black feet made square by open muddy potato-toes. Nude spherical heads of coal, with the curly leftovers of mineral hair. But their black shiny faces were caged in by the most strange steel muzzles, open-meshed like the ones on mastiffs. In the center of the muzzle, right over their doggy noses, an even stranger lock.

They looked like prison guards, and they were muzzled like wild beasts. That could have been disturbing, in any other place, as any dangerous mystery can be disturbing; but on the Dune of Camels, on the Island of the Untameables, there was no room for mystery.

Everything was clear under the merciless sunlight that would have reduced any European cranium to madness. The gallop of the heat across the flame-congested sky forewarned of the tropical noon. Enraged, the sun sparkled like a sharp smooth sword held high by a celestial executioner. Below, the terrorized isle trembled, bristling with flames like the head of a condemned prisoner. Light. Silence. Destiny.

Perhaps it was an island in the African Seas. But I doubt it. More likely, an island that had emerged from the lava sea within a volcano. The sky overhead in fact was the dome of an immense furnace. Scalding air, heavy, greasy and arid at the same time. Solar tactilism of burning scarlet sponges, sandpaper and iron brushes.

The heat was piercing. It sliced through everything from up above. Fierce. The white uniforms were blinding.

—Vokur! Wake up! I'm hungry and thirsty! shouted Mazzapà. And the yellowish cornea of his eyes shot out cruel gleams.

His companion shook himself; then slowly began to get up as if he were bearing the whole burden of the heavy noon on his back. A little way off, there was a well. Dry, of course. Farther to the right, a pile of rocks. Vokur kneeled and with great effort lifted a sandy trapdoor. He took out two yellow bowls, filled with a muddy liquid.

Vokur was thickset and stocky, fat, a little flaccid in his large, white uniform that billowed around his waist like a sail. An absurd sight it was, because the air was motionless, dead. When he got up, being very careful not to spill the contents of the bowls, his steel muzzle was beaded with sweat.

He tried with all his might not to sink his steps into the powdery, gleaming sand that gave treacherously under his big square feet. He put the bowls down on the sand, and crouched next to Mazzapà who grumbled:

—Watch the water in the bowls. Count your breaths. At the eighth breath, the water will boil.

From the harsh tone of his voice, it was obvious Mazzapà dominated his companion, roughly hewn, slow, and closed off in his primitive brutality. Mazzapà was the younger and the more agile of the two. His well-developed muscles were not affected by the torpor of the sunlight. Always ready for action, they poured sweat under his uniform, which stuck here and there to his body. Those muscles were always ready for action. His black eyes, shiny and malicious, struggled against the mandatory violence of the Sun. It wanted to hypnotize Mazzapà. It couldn't. Mazzapà scorned the Sun with his mouth which bristled full of white laughter. But suddenly his mouth tightened, as if in a fit of rage.

—Soon we'll have to feed those damned animals! he said, pointing his fist to the right, where the sands piled up to form a subsidence.

In the middle of that depression, a pit contained a mysterious tangle of large pieces of rusty metal. Looking carefully, your eyes could notice a slight fluctuation. It wasn't metal, or plants, but human bodies the color of brick and coagulated blood. Glistening sands stretched beyond that shapeless heap with breathing waviness, as if covering large, sleeping female bodies with their softness.

Here and there, some shrubs stunned by the solar heat. No shade. Beyond the pit, still to the right, the incandescent evaporation veiled an immense oasis, reddish and similar to a bronze wall that closed off the horizon.

Vokur, sitting in the sand with his legs crossed, counted his breaths on his fingers, moving his torso back and forth so as not to lose count, and he watched the two bowls as they baked in the sun.

—ffoon ffoon ffoon ffoon ffoon ffoon ffoon ffoon.

The liquid came to a boil, revealing gray beans. Then, each of the men took his bowl, and throwing his head back, poured the contents on the sizzling steel of the muzzle that caged in his gaping mouth.

—Damned job! said Mazzapà. Having to feed ourselves with this filthy, boiling broth, when we're dying from the heat.

—You're the one who wanted it hot! growled Vokur. I like it lukewarm.

—If we didn't boil it, you idiot, we'd be poisoned by now! The water under those rocks is rotten. Maybe it's the juice of a dead body. If only our comrades would come with the buffaloes and sheep. Don't you hear the noise of chains? The Untameables are getting restless because they're hungry...Vokur! Vokur! don't fall asleep again. Listen carefully. When you go to slaughter the buffaloes, remember to bring the bowls. When I shove the bayonet into their bellies, you be ready under the flow of blood. That way we'll have something decent to drink.

—No! no, Mazzapà. I won't do it. I can't do it. You know it's forbidden...The Paper People have no pity. They'd punish us by making the muzzle straps two holes tighter. I'd rather eat rot than spend two nights with my muzzle on. The other night, the Great Chief of Paper whistled in my ear: "If you so much as drink a single drop of buffalo blood, you'll be in big trouble, because it's all reserved for the Untameables. You must boil and drink the rotten water, if you want to go to the Oasis without your muzzle and enjoy the evening."

—I don't give a damn about the Oasis! We'll just keep on dying, day by day, of hunger and thirst. What's the point of going to the Oasis every night, if we can't remember anything the next day? We can't even tell what's in the Oasis. Even the Untameables don't know what they see at night. And yet, they're smart. They were all important and rich men. They talk, they talk about their past, but they can't tell what happened yesterday or the night before. Old Negodrò[†] told me this well used to be full of water! Negodrò had been to the Oasis many times. The Paper People protected him. He told me the well dried up all of a sudden. It was an awful hawk that swooped down from the sky and stayed a whole day with his wings outspread over the well. The hawk drank all the island's blood from that hole. One day, I went down into it. But I was afraid, and I climbed back out. Negodrò told me it would take ten days to reach the bottom.

—I'd be willing to walk three hundred days, if I could be sure of finding water at the bottom.

—That water's dead, Vokur!

[†] This paronomasia (*Negro*) literally means: *I shall enjoy it* or *I'm going to love this*.

A pause of silent fire. It was broken by a piercing cry. Mazzapà and Vokur turned toward their Negro comrades. Woken up suddenly, they were blubbering lugubriously. One of them stood up and was gesturing toward the Sun. It was not clear what he meant. A dark rage shook his great bony back that was decorated by his dazzling uniform decorated with slimy brown arabesques as it stuck here and there to his back.

He held his head back, so that his muzzle shone like a silver spider under the noonday sun.

He furiously battered at the muzzle and his black nose bled. He kept trying to rip it off as he yelled:

—It's biting me, it's biting me, it's biting me! A hyena is eating my face.

With his right hand, he grasped the lock of the muzzle and pulling from the front with his biceps bulging he dove headfirst into the sand. Motionless.

His comrades mumbled and lay down again. They were already sleeping with the long snore of peaceful insects.

2

THE BATTLE OF THE TWO OASES

A long pause of silent flame. Mazzapà said:

—Negodrò told me there was once a large oasis, called the Oasis of the Moon. Not as high, but deeper than the one down there that they call the Oasis of the Sun. The two oases lived next to each other, separated by a deep *wadi*. The Moon reigned happily in its thick, cool, sweet-smelling oasis, full of blue lakes and silvery streaming fugues.

"The sun, devoured by jealousy, chose to destroy it. He decided to fight it out at high noon, and unleashed his two thousand flaming solid-gold eagles.

"It was the hour when the Oasis of the Moon lies idly dozing to the clanking of the camels carrying skins full of blue water. Panic among the leaves. With a lacerat-

85

ing cry, the Oasis awakes under the assault. Immediately, it mobilizes its perfumed greenery, to defend itself. Like women, unviolated, softly fanning their charms weakness sweetness flavors and warmth of their burrows. The two thousand furious solar eagles hurled themselves downwards. But they are forced to stop. Who opposed their charge? Anguish and surprise. In reality, the first eagles have already been defeated. Poisoned by cowardice and tenderness, hesitant, played out, they tremble at the edge of the Oasis.

"Their charcoal-feathered wings are crumpled, sucked in by the gurgling of the melodious leaves. They tumble in a whirl. Others plummet like sacks of gold. Above, the more daring circle spinning like clock wheels gone mad. Most of the winged army draws back while the whole Oasis of the Moon proudly rings out.

"A brief pause. The eagles return. This time with strategic cunning. Pretending to lose themselves in delicious rapture, they sing and sob of love. They fly around the silver tree trunks on the great blue lakes. The Oasis of the Moon revels vainly, with a long sappy gurgling of fountains. Its languid and poisonous defenses are in disorder by now. The eagles, who plunge beak first into the trees, take advantage of this. A frantic shrill drilling. Their beaks burn the metal skins, like acetylene torches. Another palm falls to the ground thud, split in two. A hailing and shimmering rumble. More trees crash down mortally wounded. Others which have been decapitated die standing. Shaking. The leaves cave in and fall on the trees' corpses like women in mourning.

"Then the sun launched its simooms of plumed sand onto the defeated Oasis, to bury it completely under a splendid monotony of shovelfuls of dusty gold.— Negodrò told me that on the crest of this dune the eagles of the sun assaulted the last caravan of camels that distributed skins of blue water during the battle. Of them all, there only remained those three carcasses of camels...Look, Vokur; don't you see gold claws on the second carcass? Don't you see feathers of lava and a beak of fire?

—I don't see anything.

—Maybe, I'm out of my mind. But the island looks like an endless carcass of a camel caught in the claws of a huge eagle of fire. Those carcasses frighten me. It's as if our comrades were all dead. Who in the world ever led us to this bloody place?

—I don't know, Mazzapà.

—I feel we've been here for at least a hundred years. I never was a camel driver. I'm a soldier, that's what I am! But I think I could drive a caravan of camels.....

—Mazzapà, I have an idea.

—It's probably stupid. You never understand anything.

—You're right. I'm not intelligent. But there's something that keeps buzzing under my hair, and I keep trying to think what it is. Mazzapà, we can't stay here, on this godforsaken island.

—Well?

—You know I can handle an ax and I'm strong. The other night, while I was looking at the trees in the Oasis, down there, the idea struck me that we could cut one down, dig it out, put it in the sea, and we could leave in it.

—You really don't understand anything. At night, the trees in the Oasis are too soft and they fall apart as if they were rotten. By day, they're harder than these muzzles. How do you think you can dig that stuff out to make a boat?

—You're right, Mazzapà; but I have another idea. Every so often, the Paper People's ships come down to the roadstead with their big creaky paper sails that are all wrinkled and covered with all those black marks like an old man's skin.

—Well, I know...What do you intend to do?

—My plan isn't easy, but it's not impossible. We'll hide behind the rocks at the roadstead, and when the Paper People land we'll climb aboard their ship and leave.

—What a moron you are! Try it, and you'll see. The ship will sink under your weight. Don't you know the Paper People are lighter than dry leaves, while you can't help but let your steps be sucked in by the sand when you walk?

Vokur fell silent, struck once again by the religious awe he felt at the gliding and almost ethereal lightness of the Paper People, rulers of the island.

3

THE PIT OF THE UNTAMEABLES

Sitting with their legs crossed on the sand, the two Negro soldiers shaded their eyes with their hands, and looked at the island's azure edge which barely divided the dazzling sea of sand dunes from the real sea, no less dazzling itself.

They each vied to be the hottest, those two seas, multiplying a billion shimmering silver emerald violet sea mirrors by a billion frenetic gold X's. There against their splendor black snarls were being drawn.

—Here come our comrades with the buffaloes and sheep, said Mazzapà.

The bleating and the crushed lowing laboriously edged closer under the sheer mass of the burning silence. Suddenly to the right, a shrieking and clattering of chains echoed in the pit of the Untameables.

These chained men-beasts heard, sniffed, understood, and already savored their tasty victims by snapping and chewing ravenously at the stray moans. The noise of the chains grew. One two three hoarse voices sawed through the silence. Anger surged up toward the sky's relentless furnace.

All of a sudden, Mazzapà stood up and shouted:

—Stop shouting, you damned beasts! You scab-ridden cadavers! Mangy dogs! Do you want a taste of my bayonet?...In the name of Allah! I swear! If the Paper People, down there, hear this racket, I'll stick you through the ass so many times with my bayonet that you'll be able to use it for a sieve!

From the screaming pit there came back a brutal and biting answer:

—What bayonet! That skewer of yours fits you just right, Mazzapà, you disgusting, scrawny little sparrow!...

More virulent insults came flying out of the pit. A sardonic sneering contest.

—Yes! Yes! A sparrow! A sparrow in a muzzle cage! You're disgusting and pitiful, fancy Negro prison guards kept under lock and key.

As Mazzapà's athletic body swelled with anger, he called to Vokur.

—Come with me. Take your rifle. If I have to kill them all, the Untameables are going to be quiet. I'm afraid the Paper People will hear this infernal noise. They'll make our muzzles two notches tighter at least!

Mazzapà plunged ahead on the path that led to the pit. His rage spurred him on. But the sand restrainer of all speed forced him to slow his pace. Vokur growled behind him, he too enraged by the sand and the Untameables.

They came into view, standing tall, red-faced and disheveled. About a hundred of them. All naked, but bristling with studs like porcupines. They were wearing iron collars, like mastiffs, fortified with studs. Their calves, thighs, biceps were constricted by bands fortified with large teeth. Bands of every size. Big ones around their broad hips and barrel chests. A special, thicker iron band, with long spiral teeth around their foreheads. Some had long gray and white beards. But they were no less daring, since the rich poisons in their blood nourished them with insatiable youth. Blond and tobacco-colored beards, even though they didn't smoke. But their mouths were smoking with revenge, and the their bulging eyes spurted out from their heads.

From a distance, all these naked bodies seemed reddish or tawny. But closer inspection revealed different shades: some of them were grayish, a little soft as if they were boneless. A tall, bony man, dark red as a skinned camel. Two thin, gaunt youths showed their brown, worm-eaten muscles, and their tendons that were like the dusty strings of an old piano. Great God, for what music! Their skin was mottled brown and scaly like a fish. Others bile-green, as if they had been squeezed by their hate. Others, jaundiced and luridly arabesqued with putrid colors.

A saffron colossus. A great sulfur-colored paunch like a gold ball in the sun. They were dripping sweat faceted like precious jewels.

Their legbands, frontlets and shiny steel collars had studs decorated with shreds of bloody flesh. Human flesh that was passed from man to man in their incessant squabbles. About twenty of these men-beasts had risen to their feet. Laboriously. Overcoming the weight of the chains welded to their wrists that held the herd of Untameables together. The trampled and whining weak ones writhed between the legs of the strong. Almost all of them were the color of coagulated blood and they were covered with great open sores, on their sides, their buttocks, their arms and their cheeks. They shook like carnivorous birds between the legs of the strong ones who caged them in.

—It's them, making all the noise! said Mazzapà. Enough! Enough! you cowardly runts! Stop shouting, you damned scorpions! If you keep it up, you won't get anything to eat, anything at all.

He was answered by a pathetic yell. Then, the strong Untameables hurled themselves on top of the weak ones on the ground, and a tremendous brawl ensued.

The weight of the chains and studded collars gave the fight a terrific rhythm, since the slowness of movement contradicted the furious speed of their eyes. Fists-pistons. Chests-bellows. Bodies-bottles grabbed around the neck by drunken hands.

—I've got you, you filthy dog!

—Why are you opening your mouth like that?

And down his throat, the fist. But the teeth bite down, and the fist comes out like a sponge drenched with blood. Two giant human pliers opened against one another. To pull out the invisible nail of the soul! They interlock. Screams. "I have him! I have him tight!" A zigzagged wheezing. A cube of terror on the chest. Faces of ancient yellow boredom, scratched by cheerful lights. The heavy tedium of a lip split by a laughing wound. The mercury of hate rises in the shiny thermometers of sweaty faces. They break themselves against each other, and broken glass showers from their eyes. And the mercury of hate pours down free, never to measure again.

But sometimes a voluptuous spasm flashes in their eyes. There among the Untameables were those who were cruel wise and perverse. They relished savored looked forward to a good meal. That wound in the belly needs perfecting. A conscious wound that waits and begs, almost delirious with joy...And the wound in that belly gets three studded foreheads that are in heat. A bundle. The cumbersome and clanging chains, like the blue bells in the red-black hell of physical pain. Quick quick, their collars whet the screeching of files and padlocks, to file file seal tightly seal their souls...Otherwise!...

Mazzapà was shouting his lungs out:

—Enough! Enough! You damned scorpions! Mangy dogs! You scab-ridden cadavers!

And grabbing his rifle by the butt, he brandished it in the air, and clusters of white glints climbed, up up the barrel, right up to the bayonet. If only the sun would finally run itself through the tip, that sun, which by dint of exacting cruelty can find no victim so worthy as itself.

Mazzapà made his rifle twirl horizontally over his head, holding it by the butt, so that his fist became the hub of a rapid and cutting wheel.—Little by little the wheel lowers itself on the fuzz of the Untameables' hair eyes mouths. Greeeeng! Shhheaff! The spinning bayonet mows them down.—A hunk of red flesh spurted out, along with a bleeding eye. But the battle went on in the raised sand that kneaded that human leaven of iron-flesh-blood. A lowing spread over the sand. Black against the horizon of the white sky, the buffaloes and sheep appeared, between the flashes-bayonets-prods of the other Negro soldiers. They slowly made their way down toward the center of the pit, where Vokur awaited them with his ax raised.

At the head of the small herd, an enormous, black buffalo, laden with black magic, dripping with ancient fluvial darkness. His smoky-wall neck let his great bearded, pensive head droop almost to the glowing sand. All at once he stopped. He sensed death. The Untameables, silent. They watched. Two arm-lengths separated the buffalo's horns from Vokur's ax. It flashed, and it fell, and the black cranium which was split like a pomegranate spewed out a long long long loooowing. The Untameables' excitement flared up again. All the naked bodies strained forward against their taut chains which were screeching, they pawed the ground like restless horses. Their gaping mouths pumped out insults:

—Get out of here! Get out of here, Vokur! That's no way to butcher animals! What do you think you're doing, you idiot?! You've wasted all the buffalo's brains, and they're so good to eat. You wretch! You miserable dung farmer! Maybe you know how to kill lice, but not buffaloes! Don't you know that this is no job for you?! Leave it to us! Leave it to us!…The art of killing's not for everybody! You spoil everything, Vokur!…He's the one, the one who checks our chains every morning! Filthy damned Negroes! Serves you right…Now you're stronger than us, and you keep us in chains…But, in hell's name! separate us!…separate us! Yes! Yes! Separate us! Each of us needs his own chains! Otherwise, there's going to be trouble!…Leave us chained, yes, but separate us from each other!

Paying no attention, the Negro soldiers undressed, and, once naked, they began to cut up the buffaloes and sheep with their axes and knives.

—For Heaven's sake, we'd better keep quiet! said

one of the Untameables. So we can admire these artists at work!

The Untameables quieted down, and standing pressed together or in overturned bunches, they told their jokes by elbowing each other, and they watched Mazzapà who was directing the slaughter.—Beneath the flashing of the axes, between the Negroes' musculature, the backs of the buffaloes crumbled like black waves breaking into a froth of red horror. Terrifyyyying moans. Slimy tangles of purple guts slipped out of their gaping bellies. Hunks of white fat. Like enormous brushes, the long Negro legs scribbled on that gelatinous palette which was full of scarlet, violet and blue. Obscenely. The bearded sex was flung from the skinned bestial nakedness. Whirling. Arms wielding axes created fantastic windmills which battled a vermilion autumn forest.

The smell of blood excited the Negroes. They strode like barbarian kings over the spoils of battle. Maybe they were under the illusion of treading on knotted boa snakes, on the rigging of purple sailing ships and sails that be slackened entering a bay won in battle.

They piled slabs of meat on one side, and the bleeding skins on the other. All of a sudden, Mazzapà raised an abdomen with two hands, over his own head, and as he showered himself in blood he showed it to everybody.

—This piece is too big. It should be cut in four! Don't you know the Untameables can't use their hands?

The sun hastily cooked cooked the meat. A sharp stench of sheepskins. A sweet smell of rot dung and putrid sweat. An Untameable about forty years old, bald, with iron-gray eyes, hooked nose, inhaled it all with his mouth open, and, shaking his heavy chains with his muscular arms, he yelled:

—You're disgusting! disgusting! disgusting! royal butchers you are! I can tell you, because I'm the famous surgeon Mirmofim![†] You have spoiled some exceptional meat! Are you trying to make salami? Why are you hacking that way and botching it up? You could have asked me for advice! Imbeciles! Ignoramuses! No! no! Don't cut up that abdomen! I want it whole, whole, whole! I could tear it up just fine with the studs on my headband! And you, Mazzapà, what are you doing? Who's the idiot who put you in command? You're the dumbest of all the Negroes!...But for God's sake! there'll come a day when all of you will be chained up, and we'll be in charge! Ah! if we were only in your place, we would devour the Paper People!...Some muzzles you have! Why, I, Mirmofim, have teeth that could chew right through them, those muzzles!

Mazzapà, who was standing there supervising the soldier butchers, turned and growled at the Untameable

[†] Possible derivative of *mirmex*, Greek for 'ant'.

who was insulting him. He looked at him with a fierce frown. Clouds of black revenge passed through his eyes and anger shook his colossal body. He grabbed his rifle, which was on the ground, and suddenly bayoneted Mirmofim in the side. The surgeon was ready for him and he turned his right buttock to receive the thrust; then with bitter irony, the synthesis of ancient grudges, he said:

—I'm not young anymore, but I'm quick, still quick as you can see. You've struck me in an old wound that's scarred over. It's deep and it's lined with skin as hard as a knife sheath. It's a wound that causes no pain. A happy wound. I chose just the right place to have it done, between two muscles that had been numb for some time. Don't stop with one. You can drive three bayonets in there if you like. Try again! I like feeling your bayonet in my flesh, deep deep inside!

4

CURGUSS THE PRIEST

Mazzapà turned and gave a signal to the Negro soldiers, who began to fling meat to the Untameables. They tossed out the meat with long arching throws, spreading a new furor of blood in that pit already full of furious bodies. The hunks of meat traced parabolas against the sky glowing red like a furnace. Strange wounded birds of prey. Most of the Untameables were on their feet and tugged convulsively at their chains trying to get in front of one another in order to spear the flying meat on the points of their headbands.

There was camaraderie and friendship among these men who were so used to fighting one another. When one of them managed to spear a piece of meat on his headband or armband, he'd immediately move over to his best friend. Gripping the meat between them with the barbs on their heads, the two friends-enemies would shred it in their devouring mouths. They drank drooled red. The bloody pulp disappeared into their tough and crunching jaws.

Biting biting biting deeper deeper with teeth teeth teeth screeching teeth-lightening, big red teeth, ugly yellow teeth tearing smashing crushing hunger hunger bile spittle drunk spewed out drunk again.

Mirmofim, a sly ingenious and strong man, had caught and devoured two large pieces of meat. But after having sniffed around, up and down, since nothing good seemed to fall anymore, he began again to shout:

—Scoundrels! You cheated us today! The buffaloes were skinny and dried out from thirst just like that well. The sheep were dusty old shoeleather. The day will come. It will! It will! And in the end you'll be here and we'll be there!

—Quiet! Quiet! Be quiet, you bully! the gray beard of another fat, oval, flushed, pimply and wrinkled Untameable screamed spat at him.—You really get on my nerves, you, and your surgery! You've eaten more than all of us, and you're still complaining, you sly dog! You even stole my second piece right off my headband! Thief! You don't know who you're dealing with! I'm a powerful priest! I've had far more fun in my life than you ever did!

All the Untameables erupted.

—Yes, yes, Curguss is right!

—No. Mirmofim is right! Mirmofim is smarter than anybody. He can really claim to have lived, conquered, seen, killed, tortured.

—But Curguss is wiser, more refined.

—What! Curguss is a goatskin full of shit!

—Let's hear them both, then we'll put it to a vote. I'm betting on Mirmofim. What backbone, what muscles!

—Quiet! Curguss is going to speak.

Puffing with rage he began again:

—I've had more fun making others suffer than you ever had, ever! I want all of you to judge! Listen! I am Curguss the priest, and the women of Belgrade know me. In my own way, I have refined taste. My church was always full of women! A miraculous church that cured all the ills of women. I remember a blonde, beautiful, very pale girl. I hypnotized her, I did whatever I wanted with her. The proper way, of course. I have always despised lust. I prefer other pleasures. That little blonde was ill. Her mother, however, was even more sick. Now I remember her name: Krumi. Well, Krumi would come with her mother to the dark church every night. I'd sit between them, and they'd hug me fearfully there on the pew. "Give me a hatpin, Krumi," I'd say. Krumi would hesitate, then she'd take a pin out of her hat, but she wouldn't give it to me. I'd grab it from her. Then, in the dark, I'd stick it in her mother's side.

She'd moan. Krumi would huddle closer to me and say

"—What are you doing? What are you doing?

"—I'm curing your mother. You pray too, pray that she'll suffer more. So she can be forgiven.

"—No! No! My mother is without sin!

"—Quiet, quiet, Krumi. That is blasphemy. Your mother is full of the ugly sins of her youth. Your mother was even a prostitute. She has much to repent for. Beg me, beg me to make her suffer!

—All the while I kept pricking her mother, who, writhed with pain-fear, didn't try to get away! Krumi would get more and more excited, almost crazy. She'd keep stroking my face hysterically. Poor Krumi! She loved me so much! But I have always despised lust. I prefer other pleasures. Ah! What joy it was sticking that pin through her mother's rotten old body!...One night, after an hour of torture, I went into the sacristy, I lit an oil lamp. Then, I dropped it into a pile of sacred vestments. They caught fire. The church was closed. The two women began screaming, in terror. I calmly reached under the altar and took out two buckets of water I had put there. I put out the small blaze, while Krumi clung to me...I have always despised lust. I prefer other pleas-ures...Now I'm forced to live in chains next to this conceited most ignorant scientist. What a beast! Do you want to anatomize my shit?

Mirmofim listened to him jeering, puffing out his chest, his head thrown back contemptuously, despite the weight of the chains holding him down at the wrists. Curguss hissed his final insulting words as he thrust his big face and his dirty gray frothy beard against the surgeon's. Perfectly still, Mirmofim waited, but his ominous look began to clot. When he saw him come within range, he shot forward with surgical precision, and there goes the horns of his barbed headband.

With the blow to his face, Curguss fell. A horrible brawl. Like an octopus whose watchful tentacles are being torn again and again. Rage grew everywhere. The chains make any squabble among the Untameables spread like a disease. Two hundred raised arms bristling with sharpening studs. Not one of them had eaten enough. Hunger and hate. Tearing each other apart. Bouncing elbows amid the clawing of great red Angora cats. Their sandy breath rises like a cattail. Blood streams out everywhere. Vines with human grapes torn asunder by a hurricane. But there is no hurricane. The air is still. In the blinding glare of the sky the sun's ax can no longer be seen, only the thousand gleaming axes that shower the Untameables' tireless carnage with blows.

Mazzapà ran around the pit sticking them with his bayonet. The soldiers put their uniforms back on. Some were already moving about in their white uniforms, but they wouldn't go near the Untameables, since they feared the continuous showers of blood.

—Leave them alone! Leave them alone! shouted

Vokur. They'll kill themselves! They'll kill each other off, those filthy scorpions. So much the better! So much the better!

—No! No! Help me! You hit them too! Like me! Right in their open mouths! They'll calm down! Sooner or later they'll have to calm down! I don't want it to happen, Vokur! I don't want the Paper People to punish us! They will, they will, I'm sure of it! They won't open our muzzles tonight!...Stick your bayonet in them! You do it too!

But Vokur's called his companion at the top of his lungs:

—Mazzapà, Mazzapà, turn around. That bastard Falfar got out of his chains, and he's escaping.

The Untameables sneered scornfully.

—Stinking prison guards! Stupid Niggers! You couldn't even keep watch over a turtle. You never noticed that Falfar hasn't eaten any meat for eight days, to lose weight. Yesterday he had lost two-thirds of his weight. This morning he slipped out of his shackles.

On the glaring white sand a few yards from the top of the dune a human figure crawled on all fours. It looked like a huge yellowish lizard. It was Falfar the skeletal Untameable trying desperately to reach freedom.

—Don't kill him! shouted Vokur.

—I'll split his butt just to stop him.

Mazzapà stood up and calmly took aim with his rifle. His white uniform was dazzling. Drunk with white sparks his muzzle seemed to shoot out fat flames from the sweaty shiny coal of his cheeks. His ugly eyes shot out the red cruel spit of rifle fire.

bang bang.

—We got you, you bastard! concluded Mazzapà, and he began to walk with Vokur toward Falfar's motionless body.

Falfar lay face down, half sunk in the sand from which his swollen and bloody ass stuck out like an enormous sponge soaked in purple red.

Motionless, with just a quiver at times that sprinkled red on the sand around him.

Mazzapà and Vokur dragged him by the feet to the edge of the pit where the Untameables waited, standing upright, greatly excited.

—His pelvis is intact, declared Mirmofim. The bullet sheared off his buttock like a razor. We ought to cut it to avoid infection. Let me worry about it. It's my profession! I'll disinfect the wound with the burning sand.

Mazzapà, who guessed that Falfar's buttock would no doubt end up in the mouths of the Untameables, speared the torn flesh on his bayonet and walked off carrying on his shoulder the human skewer that he had pulled from the cannibal fire.

5

KUROTOPLAC THE SCHOOLTEACHER

In an uproar the Untameables laughed roared sneered squabbled and ridiculed the Negro soldiers. A small eel-like yellow body thrashed about most impudently, little gray eyes in a flat face with red dots like a picture spelling book. His name was Kurotoplac.

—I like your bayonets. How ridiculous these Negroes are! They truly understand nothing of blood and torture. Mazzapà, you should know by now that we enjoy ourselves carrying on like this! Everyone gets his jollies in his own way! When I was a schoolteacher in Odessa, during the time of the Czar, I used to enjoy whipping my pupils bloody to teach them respect for authority. On their bare asses, that's right, on their bare asses I'd whip them! Their asses were purple, like monkeys', like Kismika's that I stab with the studs of my headband. He takes it words in freedom screaming and loving it, the bastard! I've slit a few kids' throats, I have! I'd did things properly! Every parent had to give me a declaration relinquishing all rights on the son that I took on as a student. "If you do your homework well, you'll see your mother in three days and a special treat." Then I'd enjoy watching them. All of them bent over their notebooks writing so carefully! It was a contest. Every so often they'd look up with begging eyes. The more loving among them worked thinking of their mothers. I'd always give the prize to the hardiest and best looking ones. What joy, in their faces, when the time for their mothers' visit drew closer.

"The prizewinners would rave to their mothers about the special treat and would praise the sweet-meats. The moment they'd leave the reception room, I'd take the prizewinners by the hand and off to the cell.

"I'd visit them a couple of hours later. Then I'd slit their throats one after the other. I'd spend three or four hours on each of them.

"Their agonizing looks still held the dream of the sweet-meats! I'd bury them myself in the school garden in the lettuce and the cabbage. At night I'd take my walk over them, reading Rousseau's *Émile*. They'd be breathing there under my feet, those fresh mouths!

"On certain scorching August nights, I'd be surrounded by so many will-o'-the-wisps! What fun! I'd kick their souls around!…Those were the days! So civilized! And you, you dirty, vulgar Negroes, you want to play the moralist? We have fun in our own way! Go ahead and stick us with your bayonets! We all have wounds ready and happy to suck in the points of your bayonets like sparkling cotton candy!

6

MIRMOFIM THE SURGEON

Meanwhile, Mirmofim was busy jamming his head barbs into priest Curguss' belly.

—Phew!—he sighed.—What big hard muscles! I've never come across such hard muscles, in the abdomen! You don't realize that your muscles would be the envy of a rhinoceros! They're tougher than the ones that chipped two of my saws at the hospital in Turin ten years ago! That was no operation, but a symphony of operations! You'll love this. Listen:

"When the war broke out, my hospital was overflowing with wounded men who needed surgery after a most bloody attack. I had five bright interns then. From dawn to noon, everything went normally. But while I was having lunch, they tell me more wounded had been brought in. Corridors full of stretchers. I decide of course to share the work.

"Boys! I say to my students. Aren't you lucky! You'll have an ample opportunity to practice and to render science a service. But, please, don't be too sensitive. You must be implacably cold. Science requires a great deal of torture. Through the screams of butchered flesh, I've come to understand all the secrets of life. Operate without mercy, watch me and do as I do. You'll be testing the human body's maximum tolerance of physical pain.

"Followed by my five interns, I went into the operating room that seemed to be made of six sharp steel blades. Six wounded men were waiting for us, on the operating tables. Like an orchestra before it begins playing, we hastily tuned our instruments. I assigned the parts: one laparotomy, two amputations of right legs, one treatment of a kneecap, one amputation of a left arm. I raised my hand, and I gave the signal, and all six of us began, like an orchestra. Oh! what a rumble that orchestra made! Either without chloroform or not enough of it. I had invented new kinds of heart defects right there on the spot! So that the bodies of the six patients throbbed artistically and sang at the top of their lungs. What miraculous harmony! But I could distinctly hear the voices of the two skinny patients: they were the woodwinds in our orchestra. The great big brawny mountain trooper I was operating on made up the brass section all by himself. The two nervous ones were as lethargic as harps and violins. Suddenly the orchestra no longer pleases me. Halfway through I stop sawing my mountain trooper's leg, feign an outburst of scientific rage, snatch the scalpel from my intern's hand on the right and continue the laparotomy he was performing. This is how its done and not like that, you idiot! Then, I stop that operation before it's over, and grab the saw away from my third intern. I saw off the wounded man's arm, and scare the other two interns so much with my angry looks that they begin sawing, zigzagging with their saws, like terrified violins. Finally I remembered my mountain trooper, and when he noticed that I had grabbed my saw again, he tried, with a sudden jerk, to sit up and he bellowed: You bastard! You bastard!

—Then, I pretend that I'm having a horrible fit of nerves, I give him a punch on the nose, and start yelling: "Don't you know I could kill you, you idiot?"

—My patient fell back flat on the table, and he closed his eyes, exhausted. I cut off his right leg, thoroughly convinced it wasn't necessary...What madness! While I was sawing a song came to mind. I think I still know it by heart:

> *Big big*
> *is the boat*
> *where our friends and family*
> *are as happy as can be*
> *when the Angelus is heard*
> *on the sea.*

In a dither
my good mother
throws a cover
on my sister who's so dear:
she's a-coughing and we fear
the cold black night
might take her far from here.

"Preacher! Preacher! Do you like this lullaby? If you do, I'll reward you by sticking you through the paunch again. Listen. The third verse:

Sister, sister
what a perfect
melancholy night!
Yet our mother was in tears
when she saw
that on the boat
death was sitting oh so near...

"With his eyes wide open the mountain trooper followed my arm sawing his leg and I could feel the song laughing in my nerves. I was just about whistling it. Of course, even though he was a stupid beast, the trooper must have sensed my joy when the saw got stuck, and he shut his eyes in terror in the face of my satanic delight:

Sister, sister
what a perfect
melancholy night…"

7

THE PAPER SAILING SHIPS

The sun was setting, but the heat seemed to be increasing. Now and then the air pulsed as if stirred by a tired breeze that had come from afar.

The Negro soldiers were no longer paying attention to the Untameables nor to their monotonous and spasmodic agitation which was subsiding. The Negro soldiers standing around Mazzapà looked at one another, worrying about the gory stains that arabesqued their white uniforms.

—What a mess we've made! said Mazzapà. There'll be trouble if the Paper People see us like this! "Uniforms are white and must stay white!" the Paper People hissed, last night. "They must be so white that every pen will be tempted to write love poems on them!"

What's the meaning of these words? I don't know...It doesn't matter! Let's go.

The Negro soldiers set out after Mazzapà in the direction of the sea. The sand was less scorching now under their squared feet with their huge toes spread apart. Their heads lowered, their torsos bobbing up and down, they were watching some big ruby-like giant red ants that began to enliven the placid brilliance of the desert.

The sea embraced the scorched island with its endless shimmering lava. Even as it was setting, the sun poured down billions and billions of rays laden with gold. A fan of red-hot perpendicular tubes that angled off the massive surface of the blue gold sea, and then converged horizontally against the island.

The island was pierced perpendicularly by direct rays and, horizontally, by reflected rays.

In the bay, between the black rocks, the dance of mirrors. Going mad! On the gravel, liquid indigo. Boiling! The Negro soldiers take off their blood-stained uniforms. They don't need to be soaked. Just let them float for a moment and they'll be whiter than snow. They're scalding hot.

Satisfied with this the soldiers put their uniforms back on, and set out again. But a rustling of dry leaves worried them as they uncorked their feet from the deep sand!

Of course the Paper People had already left their

distant bronze oasis. The rustling could be heard again. Then stopped. Silence reigned sovereign. Mazzapà said:

—Fortunately, the Untameables have quieted down. They're not shouting anymore. Now, they're not yelling. It figures: after all that bayoneting! But unfortunately they'll wake up again! I wouldn't want the Paper People to punish us on account of those dogs. Let's go. Just to make sure, let's give them an extra dose of our bayonets. This muzzle is killing me. I can't stand it anymore...Vokur, what a hellish day this is! Take the path to the left, and head for the Paper People. Hurry up. Try to hold them up for a while, with your daily report. I'm going to the pit. Those animals could begin their racket all over again, you never know. You tell the Great Paper Chief that if they heard shouting today, it wasn't our fault. We can't satisfy the Untameables, with those scrawny buffaloes. How come the Paper People insist on sending us such skinny animals? They must have some fat ones, in the parks, at the end of the Oasis. The Untameables need a lot of hardy food. Otherwise, one of these days they'll break out of their chains and eat us up! Then they'll eat the Paper People too.

Vokur took to the path with a slow pace. The rustling grew, and it granulated the silence. It spread. It became more intense. The air seemed like it had been chewed up, perforated by that noise. As if endless crackling and screeching cracks were opening in the vault of the sky. Rubbing and creeping, the noise expanded along the still-feeble breeze that seemed to test its strength against the thickness of the air.

When he and the soldiers got to the top of a dune overlooking the pit, Mazzapà stopped to take a look around. Down to the right, the Untameables were slumped on one another and they had reorganized their tragic mechanism of intermeshed bodies, an enormous yellow hedgehog bristling with flesh, steel and rusty iron.

The infinitesimal rustling was growing louder, as if a wind laden with dead leaves had arisen. It was the typical sound that the Paper People made. A dune hid them from Mazzapà's sight. He squinted his eyes. He spotted them. They were swaying very gently, sweeping across the sand, in their yellow cone-shaped robes that were lined with writing. Each wore a circumflex hat that was formed by an open black book turned upside down. They were within twenty paces of Mazzapà on the dune overlooking the pit.

There are eleven of them, in single file, all taciturn. They watch with gray flat eyeless faces and with open mouths shaped like zeros or Oh's of amazement.

They hissed:

—Good! Bad! You're wrong! Right! Duty and guilt! You tame the Untameables and you take orders from us, so that the Great No One neither takes charge nor takes control! You are Negroes, imprisoned prison guards, and you deserve our rambling approving-scorn!

You will be punished or rewarded. And who knows, in a while, we may decide to not open your muzzles!

While they spoke, a meticulous wind did nothing but stir the hems of their paper cone-shaped robes that were lined with writing and printing. The surrounding air remained still. In the center of the pit, the Untameables had sunken into a most heavy sleep. They snored and sizzled in the pit—Sssssuu hrrrrr Sssssuu hrrrrr—in the fat of their scars like fish piled in a frying pan too small. The sun was setting on the sinuous profile of the great bronze Oasis that seemed, however, to grow tender at the edges and to lose its mechanical stiffness under the brighter light.

Facing the other side of the island, three small brown clouds stood out against the arc of the sea's horizon. Round at first. Then they opened up like black petals. They were not clouds and they were not black, but the sun, which was still high, made them black. Finally they revealed that they were really tall masts full of sails. The first turned pale. They were three sailing ships with sails as yellow as a canary. All around the high sea rejoiced in them. Or rather that inferno of molten gold gloried in them. A vibrant ecstasy of alert gold faces. A frenzy of golden bees. An endless loom of frenetic gold. A hundred thousand nets laden with crazed fish. A deifying shower of diamonds. The three yellow sailing ships cruised placidly with ceremonious arrogance and slow bows. Each of them had a terrifying lividness about their keels. Then the tallest of the Paper People hissed:

—Let us go and receive the orders of our King, Emperor, God: His Majesty the Contradictor.

Across the sand that the setting sun was turning into saffron, the eleven Paper People slipped away, one behind the other, eleven yellow swirling cones.

The high sea multiplied its ever-changing marvels: zinc and silver plates with soft blue and flesh-tinted veining, maudlin glances and swooning turquoise stones. As it grew more lively and gay, the inferno of molten gold was ready to assault those skeptical and austere sailing ships. They looked like monstrous tropical flowers tormented by buzzing liquid gold bees. The immense gold loom of the high sea shuddered as it wove sails even more beautiful for those splendid ships! A light hesitant breeze wandered about with a thousand slippery, cool, metallic tactilisms, made of silver paper, smooth silk, ermine and chinchilla. But, at times, the air held in its breath, and the three ships would sail on under their own wind that filled the taut canvases, without stirring anything else. Now one could clearly see all the parts of the remarkable ships. The three keels were actually made of brown leather. Not riveted, but sewn and fastened with studs of ancient gold. In some wondrous shipyard, perhaps one of the ports of the moon, expert caulkers had sewn together the leather bindings of nine thousand ancient books, fashioning thus three solid but flexible keels, better than any other ship's keel, because they conformed to the yielding flesh and capricious eyes of the sea.

The yellow sails lined with writing and printing creaked, creaked as they billowed out like starched skirts, or books of empty philosophy.

The three ships came to a halt with a light pitching and rolling, but their sails remained filled, perhaps with pride at what they were carrying. The eleven Paper People stood in a row on the shore, silent and motionless. Bobbing gracefully the three ships lined up with their bowsprits pointed to the shore. On each bowsprit could be seen a Paper Person identical to the ones waiting below. Each with his circumflex book-hat and his yellow cone-shaped robe lined with writing and printing. All three opened their mouths in an Oh of amazement. The first one hissed:

—ZERO.

Between the first and second ships, the sea gurgled:

—More, more, more, more...

The second Paper Person, on the second ship, hissed through his amazed-Oh mouth:

—ZERO.

The sea, between the second and third ship held out the word:

—Saaaaaaame...

The third Paper Person, on the bowsprit of the third ship, hissed:

—ZERO.

Suddenly, the eleven Paper People on the shore turned their backs to the ships, and slipping away like cone-shaped whirling sand, they reached the dune overlooking the pit of the Untameables.

8

UNLOCKING THE MUZZLES

The sun had disappeared behind the Oasis that was dilating in the sky, an immense rosy and resonant seashell.

The Untameables were all standing, their heads thrown back, with wide open defiant eyes, all of them silent.—The warm breeze wrapped them in its sweet morphines. They were already under its spell when the Chief of the Paper People murmured:

—Let the locks be opened.

The Negro soldiers went down into the pit, at once, and without taking any precautions they began to release the Untameables from their chains.

The light was a voluptuous and iridescent cream. The air was plumed and pliant, as if full with the softest springs. An aerial exciting warm tactilism longing for velvet and wool crepe. Now and then the breath of the sun, with its grainy silks and warm sponges. The sand no longer inflated their footsteps. The numberless, red and shiny giant ants embellished the silky flesh of the sand, like rubies. When the Untameables had all been freed from their chains, Mirmofim, expanding his chest with a single breath, said in a jovial and paternal voice:

—Ah, what a beautiful Sunday night with the family!

A dawning of cordiality cooled the faces of the Untameables, while the Paper People slipped hurriedly among the Negro soldiers, and unlocked their muzzles, with the white flash of their ivory arms out of their cone-shaped robes.

As they began to walk in single file, their muzzles gently clinked like happy pebbles in the stream of their march. Ahead of them, the Untameables scurried along, joked, and gestured like schoolboys out for a walk. On the right, on the left, the Paper People guided them, like kind-hearted schoolmasters, and the rustling of their conical paper robes accompanied the clinking of the muzzles and the studded collars that no longer hurt them, but decorated their naked bodies like elegant jewels.

This is how the college of pacified Untameables made its way, toward the Oasis of divine wet and dark holidays.

The Untameables walked for a few minutes calmly

and carefree. The joy of being able to move detached from one another made them forget the weight of the chains that they were carrying coiled on their backs, resonant knapsacks. On their skin they savored the fresh velvets of the night and they stretched their cheeks, still contracted in anger, to sketch their first strenuous smile.

But they contorted their faces clumsily and could not achieve the desired expression. Some of them let loose and invented semi-cruel pranks. Like schoolboys, they tripped each other or danced about and amused themselves with the resonant clattering of the muzzles. But as soon as they felt the blue-green breath of the great Oasis, they became silent.

With eyes wide-open they admired the immense green wall of giant trees that majestically unfurled its tide of leaves more than a hundred meters from the ground.

They were still far from the trees, when they found themselves in the enchanting and maternal shadow of the Oasis.

Mirmofim, the surgeon, the ever-unpredictable orchestral spirit among them, began to sing his favorite song:

> *Big big*
> *is the boat*
> *where our friends and family*
> *are as happy as can be*
> *when the Angelus is heard*
> *on the sea…*

The Untameables wanted to sing too. They tried to harmonize, but their harsh voices were broken by sobs shrieks raucous outbursts and comic wrong notes. The result was an atrocious cacophony.

—Keep quiet! shouted Mirmofim.—Let me sing alone. You're all off key!

Mirmofim broke into the third stanza, all caught up in the arrogant pride of a singer:

> *Sister, sister*
> *what a perfect*
> *melancholy night...*

—Melancholy night my foot! You really get on our nerves, you weakling! burst out Curguss the priest, as he puffed under the weight of his pack of chains.—We need cheer! cheer!

—But I feel like being sad! sad!

—And I feel like being cheerful!

—And I sad!

—I, cheerful

—Sad! sad!

—This is neither the time nor the place for sadness!

—And this is neither the time nor place for cheer! Phooey!...

And Mirmofim, with a powerful backhand slap knocked the priest to the ground.—A fight. A fierce tangle of bodies. Untangle. A tighter tangle. Intermingling of flesh and sand. Tumbling. A crush of rage. In the swirling dust, the Negro soldiers howled like jackals. Kicking and punching to separate them. They all were arguing about the brawl. No one understood.

Vokur gave out some kicks, bloodying himself on the barbed armbands and legbands of the Untameables.

—The Paper People have disappeared! shouted Mazzapà. They've deserted us! We don't know the way. Without them, how are we going to get into the Oasis? It's your fault! you damned Untameables!

A mysterious terror ran through the column of men who were already fraught with squabbles and bestial rage. Their outcries ceased. All of them motionless, gripped by the tragic anxiety that came from the dark and menacing Oasis.

The pallor of the sky had turned gray, and down there, at five hundred paces between the trunks of the gigantic trees, you could hear the sinister creaking of numberless locks perhaps like the ones that fastened their chains. It reminded the Negro soldiers of their muzzles. They were all trembling. But suddenly the surgeon came up with an idea:

—Let's go, let's go, and no more fighting! he said to the priest.

And he put out his hand to help him up. The priest was muttering something. Anger sputtered in his throat. But he got up, and they all took to the road. Immediately, as if by magic powers, the sky reopened its white roses of peaceful sweetness.

9

THE OASIS

The Untameables advanced into the complaisant shadow of the Oasis. They could barely see, but all felt reassured. Vokur, who had moved to the head of the column in order to lead it better, called to Mazzapà:

—Look! This must be the right path.

In fact the path was outlined as if layered with a phosphorescent glow.

—The tracks of the great snails!

—Great snails my foot! There aren't any snails, in the Oasis! You're the snail-brain here! answered Mazzapà. Those are the luminous tracks of the Paper People...You'll see! You'll see!

From the vegetal shadow, down there, where the

z z z z z z z z z z z z z z z z z z z z z z z z z z z z z z z z z

vaguely silvery path wound its way, there came a
z z z z z z z z z z z z z z z z z z z z z z z z z z z z z z z z
noise-sound kind of like the rustling of the Paper
z z z z z z z z z z z z z z z z z z z z z z z z z z z z z z z z
People's robes, but softer. It bubbled and gurgled like
a fresh spring in love. The path wound its way through
mounds of cacti and agaves, athletic warriors armed
with lances ready to defend the dense colonnade of palm
and sycamore trees. A warm human air with the
tactilism of suede and horsehair.

The vegetation grew thicker and its shapes went crazy
in the nightmare crucible of darkness.

The gigantic and bewildering cacti and agaves dominated everything. From above they seemed like kings
at rest after a battle. But below, the battle of the vegetal
shapes had already begun again with renewed violence.

Monstrous cacti and agaves, like shredded elephants
and rhinoceroses, crushed by attacking crocodiles with
their huge shears twisting in their mouths.

Witchcraft of light! They were not crocodiles, but
perhaps actual monumental shears of fabulous garden-
ers bent on bringing order to that untameable flora. Non-
sense! who would dare offend the venerable divinity of
primeval disorder with the thought of man's wretched
art of gardening?

Cacti and agaves were really hands cut from giants
bound in rusty chains. Bizarre matches of cricket and
lawn-tennis broke out merrily bristling with rackets.

Flight of rapid legs squirting fruits-balls into the air. But nobody was running. Everything was petrified. Spikes or spires? Towering metallic. Shadowy sieves of bronze dripping with the foam from prisoners' faces. On the right monsters escaping. On the left more crocodiles half-buried in the mud. And really it was a duel between a hundred camouflaged cacti and agaves.

With the proud flickering slenderness of sharks the agaves attacked the cacti, lunge, parry, disengage, lunge.

Above, a gallery of hideous hands broke out motionless in a petrified applause. Higher still, the great phalluses of the agaves were erect and ready to deflower and they were swelling with their bold lust for the stars.

The gnarled cacti meanwhile had fallen into a defensive formation and they laughed a thousand of their Negro laughs and jeered at the agaves that threatened them from all sides. The latter, who were green swordsmen, were showing off the springs of their biceps, arching out their metal necks and rubber torsos, but they dared not hurl themselves on the cacti, perhaps because they were so elegant that they were leery of those lurid Negro shapes.

Below, a darkness rife with perfume gave shape to a wide black and thick river in which the Negro cacti were slaughtering all those sinister crocodillic agaves with blows from their oars. The more daring of them stood waist-deep in the water killing the resilient green jeweled octopus with emerald daggers.

Above, the crest of the Oasis sagged at times like a bed under the weight of an invisible, immense nude woman. There wafted about the perfume-memory of a night of love that had lasted a hundred years. With their eyes, their cheeks, their mouths, the Untameables and the Negro soldiers turned their heads as they marched so as to take pleasure in the fresh aerial sea of overhanging leaves.

Baaaack foooorth, uuuup dowwwwn, drenched with a sweet indolence, the leaves sought to perfect the grace of their undulating rhythm.—The path turned toward the fleshy tenderness of the jasmine and acacias, and suddenly three large trees heaved wide open just like a cottage in the woods is wont at times to open its warm heart to the wayfarer in the storm.

A Paper Person appeared in each tree, but they were lighted from within, and quite different from those seen before.

Their paper cone-shaped robes lined with writing and printing seemed like translucent glass on their agile bodies which were red like flame turned upside-down.—The stunned Untameables came to a halt between admiration and fear. But, perhaps by some magic of those bodies of flame an increasingly compelling and persuasive music spread from the translucent robes enticing them to move on, and the column set out again.

More Paper People sprang out from the other trees, and as these marvelous flitting lanterns multiplied, the Untameables and the Negro soldiers entered the Oasis, now sure they were being led toward a paradise of imagination.

The surgeon and the priest were in front. Now they weren't the least bit afraid. They wanted to see. They were the wisest of them all. One day they would be able to tell all about it. But others wanted the honor of exploring and being the first, the first to see.

—I'm a schoolteacher, said Kurotoplac elbowing his way forward.—I know music. I can explain to you the harmony of the forest better than anyone. I'll walk ahead of everybody, since the shuffling of your feet is distracting me.

—Well, that's all we need! the surgeon muttered sarcastically.—You were just singing like a broken teakettle, and you've worn out your eyes reading too many books. You can't hear nor see a thing. With you we'd lose our way again.

—Quiet! Quiet, for God's sake! said the priest. Let's not start quarreling again! Haven't you noticed that the minute one of us raises his voice to argue, the music of the leaves dies down; and, what's worse, look!…The glowing Paper People turn off and disappear. Let's walk silently and orderly, without dragging our feet. I know what the dark's about. I feel my soul welling up with prayer. It's like being in church!

—Damn your church! ripped in the surgeon.—Why don't you just give it up!

The path grew dark again, the music died down, and in the silence only the chains and muzzles could be heard, since everyone, soldiers and Untameables alike, were trembling.

A long pause of dark terror. A flapping of wings. A thud. A timid confession of humble and stuttering light against the confessional grating of the leaves. Then a white spasm, and the wandering flames reappeared, and the musical fountains once again wove their tempos, at times jumpy cold like spurts, at times stepping down into the large rhythms of foliage that dreams of flying.

The olive trees, the fig trees, the banana trees lazily fashioned beds and hammocks out of shadows. They've already changed shape. Fleeting breezes with a female body hollow them out. Now they're becoming blue naves which lose themselves obliquely in the depths of the Oasis.

The path became less irregular. More and more like silver, it wound its way as if it were the luminous vein of a great heart bubbling with white light at the center of the Oasis.

With a melodious tinkling, a brightly lit Paper Person bigger than the others popped out from a thicket on the right.—He stopped for a moment on the path, twenty paces from the column. Then he began to run around it. The upside-down red flame of his body was already being fanned by a steady wind, while his transparent cone-shaped robe whirled madly in the direction opposite to his gliding motion.

Despite his speed, one could clearly see the characters printed and written on his robe. The Untameables, who had stopped, remarked upon this with amazement.

As the Paper Person rapidly ran a second time around the column, the priest said:

—I've got good eyesight! I'll figure it out. Watch!

The great Paper Person spun by, a red flash in the dark.

—I did it, said the priest.—On his robe it says: "God is waiting for you on the shore of the lake. All drought ends in the lake."

—We don't believe you! said the surgeon. That's just a priest's trick for the country bumpkin. But on the other hand, I'm thirsty too. Let's go.

The great Paper Person ran ahead, and the Untameables followed him and penetrated further into the Oasis. All arguing had stopped. Each was striving to change the expression on his face, still deeply lined by all the old vengeful grimaces. Each was praising his companion, extolling his virtues, his refined qualities, his goodness. They joked awkwardly as they tested and re-tested the impossible tenderness that they found in their voices and their gestures. Their voices and gestures were crooked disjointed aslant foaming with ancient bile.

From the right came the faint tinkling of a distant caravan. It grew louder. Then died down.

There's the sound again, louder. Its faint glitter hangs in the dark. It turns into a tremulous gold arabesque and dances dances among the tree trunks.

Enchanted, the Untameables stop, and right away the bright and resilient arabesque uncoils to give birth to hundred and hundreds and hundreds of gold spirals streaming with little bells. They are living gold spirals that sing like a mist in a fairy-tale twilight:

I am a Little Spiral.
They call me Queeraling
And you? and you? and you?

They call me Pragmonic.
And you? and you? and you?

They call me Little Quail.
And you? and you?...

Cheer ful ful
Cheer ful ful
Cheerful Cheerful Cheerful.

I love I smoke I shake.
We are were and will be
the perfume supreme
a-thinking
in the forest
at its crest.

Shakì smokì lovì
Smòprasu smokiprò
Nowha
Stathee
Beoutthe tra la la

10

VEGETAL HARPS

They vanished. Silence.

Now, the silvery path winds among gigantic tangles of towering lianas that hang from trees. Strange white glints drip down the listless vines. The music begins again, but so oppressive with its sweetness and desperate tenderness, that the surgeon turned suddenly to the priest and muttered:

—Do you believe in the infinite benevolence of God?

The priest did not answer, absorbed as he was in the wonderment growing all around him. The endless tangle of lianas became more and more unpredictable. They did not look like lianas anymore, but like loosened strings of gigantic harps. An infinite number of strings overwhelmed by the overflowing sweetness of sound. A sound made of a thousand sounds that crept up on the brain and immensified it.

The strange white glints on the liana that seemed like drops of pure sap began to leap about, and their movement gave rhythm to the music of the Oasis.

—Those white things aren't sap! said Mazzapà.— They're white birds!

Long white birds with shiny silk plumage were flying around at about eye level, and not by chance, but deliberately, they hit or brushed against the lianas, drawing from them a vast polyphony of crystals and handbells that broke up into moaning chords and ever changing cascades of endlessly tremulous notes. Confused, perhaps, one of the birds began to fly, grazing the heads of the Untameables. Perhaps in its musical rapture it hoped to draw out a new sound from the sharp points of their headbands.

The bird's artistic delirium amused the column. They all laughed, competing to offer their barbed heads to the strumming plumes of that winged musician.

—What strange claws, they're coral! Look! Its beak is a turquoise hook, pronounced the schoolteacher.

The bird swooped back even lower. With inspiration. It brushed the thorns on those evil foreheads which were showing signs of goodness under the aeroliquid tinkling, as if baptized anew in a river of good.

The musical birds were multiplying. They came in such white swift flocks that they seemed like the rays of an even swifter moon. But there was no moon. There was however the longing, the hope, the memory, the yearning for a new moon invented by poets.

The bold arches of the Oasis were thrilled by the white trepidation of flight and music, as if something superhuman were about to appear.

—Everyone stop, and have a look! shouted Mazzapà. —There are those blue titties. I have seen them before. There were a lot of them, in the Oasis of the Moon.

They all crowded around Mazzapà, who kneeled in the grass and pointed to a strange little beast that looked like a dark blue breast, with six coral legs.

Wonder and anxiety weighed heavy on the chests of the Untameables, and it was Thirst, that ancient thirst for knowledge that had scorpioned itself in their bellies, in their lungs for such a long time. But it had been transformed, purified, it was almost spiritual.—They felt that soon they could quench their thirst forever. A tickling and vaporous coolness rained down from the trees. Transparencies of honey and perfumed oils dripped down.

Joyously, the Untameables exposed their wounds to the balms and ointment that impregnated the air.—A fantasy! A fantasy! They are neither balms nor ointments! It's the merciful music that penetrates the flesh and anoints it with pity. They are balmy lights that ease the torture of the sores.

In their mouths, on their tongues, on their foreheads

and all their wounds, the Untameables were deliciously dying of thirst, thirst, thirst, thirst, thirst.

It was like the thirst that had been caressed and squeezed from the waves of music. It became the thirst for an ever-more vast, throbbing, consoling chord. It was the great Thirst for icy spirituality and humid goodness. It sang, it cried, it tore itself apart, and rising, rising on the great lianas strummed by the birds, it sobbed, sobbed desperately, toward the sky, that Thirst Thirst stronger than any Thirst! And the Lake appeared.

11

THE LAKE

Motionless and resplendent, a velvety splendor somewhere between white and blue, with infinite smiles of
innocent children swimming in the silver water. No one
was swimming in that motionless water; but its surface
rippled now and then with fleeting apparitions. Gentle
profiles of evanescent women, curves of exquisite nude
bodies, misty locks of hair, fingers adorned with rings...

There was nothing in that lake, nothing. But all
dreams bubbled sweetly there among velvets crystals
and melodious jewels.

The lake was motionless and issued no sound. It
poured out instead its blissful splendor, nourishing the
immense growths of liana and gigantic palms with its
bounty of light, the way the heart nourishes the body's

forest with blood as if its trees were bones and arteries, and its leaves were trembling flesh.

The lake was no less than twenty kilometers wide, yet it was as intimate and personal as a bathtub. It was alive, it breathed, dreamt of a thousand metamorphoses. It would have shrunk to a puddle under the feet of a child. Had it wished to do so, it could have easily pushed aside its towering walls of resonant liana, and invaded the Oasis, drowning it the way intense sweetness drowns sweetness already tasted.

The winding shores of the lake were deserted, but they had a thoughtful and sour harshness about them and they had the heartfelt solitude of prehistoric caves combined with the breathing quality of present artistic genius. Primordial and utterly modern shores, far away and present, dreamt about and lived through. They obeyed and escaped the creative will of those who gazed at them. The air was an uncertain caress of silk velvet peach down and bird feathers.

The lake seemed like hypnotic underwater moonlight painted by a diver artist. Moonlight dripping from the heart of a wild poet. It was spellbinding like a great work of art. Projected against the high vault of the night sky, this spell had unleashed and enraptured the constellations, and the stars, now released from one another, flew about like red ribbons, blue diamonds, gold insects, fire ivy, hooks sparkling with joy, vermilion mouths, knots of burning coal, clusters of emeralds, ruby doves in total freedom.

The stars in freedom flew and darted over the slippery lake of tempered moonlight.

Mirmofim, the first to arrive at the shore, was the first to observe the miracle.

—They've even freed the stars from their chains! No more, no more constellations lined-up like prisoners! The stars are free! We've found the Lake of Freedom at last.

Eleven Paper People sprang up on the other side, luminous cones whirling with a silky buzz.

The tallest one spoke:

—This is not the Lake of Freedom. You've reached the Lake of Poetry and Feeling! Drink up, bathe, and create, if you can, with the coolness of these waves, the high serene music of Goodness.

While he was talking more luminous Paper People arrived. By the hundreds. They flowed and flowed from the depths of the Oasis to the shore.

Mirmofim counted them. There were three hundred. But he tired of counting them because by then the other shore was thick with Paper People who each shined in the whirling cone of his colored robe.

They looked like a mechanical tribe of thinking lamps crowded together in a circle for a show on the lake which was half lit by the vigor of their own light. The other half kept the placid candor of its lunar silver.

The great Paper Person raised his voice:

—Untameables! don't be afraid of evil spells! Bathe yourselves in these beneficent waters and make soft music out of love. I know the savage cruelty of all the poisons that run in your veins. I know the accursed deafness of your fossil heads. But in this water you'll find the art of vibration and woven sound. I shall not counsel you. If you're uninspired, look through our robes, and right away you'll find the notes you need. We'll be your judges. When you achieve the great human rhythm, we'll lead you to the stupendous City of Spiritual Freedom!

That fool Vokur dove into the water right away, crudely breaking the surface with the mass of his Negro body. They all made fun of him. But the Negroes were already following his example, and they quickly undressed, while the Untameables continued to wait.

12

THE LAST CACOPHONY

Mazzapà's coal-black athletic musculature dripped with blue-white reflections, as he gesticulated anxiously to Mirmofim, inviting him to bathe. Finally he took him by the arm, and he dragged him into the water which broke with a moaning chord.

Pushing and rolling over each other, the others went in and joked and argued with the glitter of that liquid light.

—This water is too beautiful for me!... You're too affectionate! Beautiful water! Beautiful water! My lady, duchess, princess, queen, water goddess! What beautiful jewels! And so many of them! Who stole them for you? You're a woman! Woman! Woman! Yet I know there aren't any women on this island! But you are woman! I wish to embrace you. Will you let me? Let me embrace you!

Everyone happily enjoyed the water as it multiplied its fleeting cool lusciousness and its thousand offers-refusals of breasts bellies arms mouths.

—I'm going to dive into your heart, my Lake, shouted Curguss. The lake is a font of holy water. Look! Look! I'm diving, I'm diving, and I bet I can stay underwater for twenty minutes, longer than a hippopotamus!

Everyone clapped. A jury was named on the spot. Curguss had dived in and was under water.—Childish wonder in all those eyes watching the surface of the water. Curguss was staying under! But the ones who could not see sneered, laughed, and pushed each other. The jury wavered. In the end they fell on Curguss who surfaced puffing like a hippopotamus.

By this time all the Untameables were in the lake and could feel its healing freshness in their wounds. They were grateful to have more mouths to drink more water.

Mirmofim the surgeon took Curguss the priest by the hand, Curguss took Kurotoplac the teacher by the hand, Mazzapà and Vokur joined them, and the five of them began a ring around the rosy in the water which en-circled them at the waist. The studs of their armbands and frontlets collided with a humble, desolate clinking sound. Now they all wanted to dance like that. The water's idle jewelry restrained the impetus of their legs. The best they could do was a slow marching step.

—I don't like it, this way! said Vokur. It feels like I'm still sinking in the sand, near the bloody pit. Come on! let's go faster.

Below, with a thousand careless fingers the water strummed sobs sighs whispers murmurs and gurgled songs invitations sucking and sucking up kisses, licking and licking up tears trinkets bon-bons rosaries tiny cascades, pearls and tail-wagging, castanets, crystals and faint bursts of laughter.

—Damn! said Mazzapà.—If we only had a banjo or a darabukka!

He left the ring around the rosy, and he got out of the water. Standing on the shore, he called to Vokur and the other Negroes. They unwillingly abandoned the delights of the water and gathered around their leader, who began to shake the chains piled among the trees.

—Really, those Negroes aren't such bad dogs after all! said Mirmofim, laughing. Sure they're ignorant, but I don't hate them as much as I used to, I hardly hate them at all! It's not their fault. They've been sentenced to be our guards, and we're not the most tame people. Sometimes I think they're too easy on us!...Vokur! Vokur! let's make a circle with all the Untameables, and we'll sing together.

—Impossible! said Kurotoplac; we don't have any instruments and we don't know any songs

—I can sing you a song, said Mirmofim. You know it, but you don't like it.

Everybody shouted:

—No! No! we do like it! It's beautiful, really beautiful! Let's try to sing it together!

The great ring around the rosy stopped. More than a hundred Untameables took each other by the hand. The new human chain they formed was so far from the sad chains that were now merely playing a barbaric and monotonous accompaniment to the naïve music of which they dreamt.

The Negroes stubbornly continued to ruckus about on the shore. Armbands legbands and studded frontlets clinked like a marching band in the lunar softness shining on the lake. In the center, Mirmofim the surgeon conducted the orchestra and sang:

> *Big big*
> *is the boat*
> *where our friends and family*
> *are as happy as can be*
> *when the Angelus is heard*
> *on the sea.*

But he stopped.

—No! no! enough with this marching beat. It smacks of war prison and cruelty and chains. Can't you hear how they clash? The song is sad and sweet. Stop your clatter, Mazzapà! Let's try the last verse, the one you don't know. I'll sing and you accompany me slowly and pretend you're insects buzzing:

zeeee…zeeee…zeeee…

Do you get it? All together! Careful now! I'll sing:

> *Death is sweet*
> *when the night winds swell*
> *the trembling sail*
> *white shroud*
> *on a dying white sea.*

The ring around the rosy began again. It was dragged out and slower on the zeeee, zeeee, zeeee's…coming from their mouths, the got got gloogloo chiaf cheef cloc plee plee plee from the water, the clinking of their frontlets while on the shore the zeen zeen zan zan the Negroes beating the chains and muzzles didn't let up.

—Enough! enough! shouted Mirmofim.—We're truly unworthy of the Paper People's friendship. We're making one hell of a racket without achieving the least musical effect. It would be better to keep quiet. At least we could enjoy the white birds' sweet music and the lianas' harps and the leaves' guitars and the song of stars in freedom. Be quiet, for God's sake! Be quiet! Listen!

13

THE VEGETAL ORCHESTRA

They fell silent, and the forest immediately intoned a
majestic chorus. Far above the stars began to sing, and
from one side of the Oasis the curvy fickle arpeggios of
the liana's great harps rose with their song. Then the
singing ebbed languidly, as if gently springing on the
tide of leaves. But just then the branches awoke among
the leaves like frantic violin bows. Up and down with a
feverish touch on the strings they squeezed all the vo-
luptuousness out of the night air.

How sweet this last phrase! That's it, that's what awak-
ens all the leaves of the great baobabs. All the leaves
are playing, countless leaves, piercing clarinets and
winged flutes, and the trees offer their organ pipes to
the high winds that race down them and come out

through the roots from round holes, with long lowing underwater notes, full of torment, threats, rapture and fortune.

Mirmofim said:

—Listen! listen! how marvelous! We must swim in this water. Let's all swim, and while we're swimming, we'll try to follow the rhythm of this supernatural music.

The Untameables began to swim, and as they swam caressed by the ethereal music, they softened their gestures and they trained for meekness. And for the first time their jagged and fanged souls dreamt of a brotherly embrace.

In gusts of music, the nightingales appeared in the high leaves over the lake. With their trills trills trills trills trills, they started a competition. They arrogantly forced all the musicians of the Oasis to raise their voices and bring the chorale to perfection by lifting it to a more intense musical light:

got got got geets   got got got got got got got got
got got got got got got geets[†]
gotyu gotyu gotyu gotyu gotyu yuuuu
yudon yudon yudon yudon yudon yuddading
gagagagagagagagagagagagagagagagagagagagagagagagaga

[†] In its original form (*tio tio...tix*), this representation of singing birds perhaps alludes to Giovanni Pascoli's poem "Nozze," and ultimately to Aristophane's "The Birds."

—It's the jittery gallants of Light! said Mirmofim.

—Gallants! gallants! gallants! sang the Untameables

got got got got got got got got got got got got got got got got

at the top of their lungs, imitating the nightingales who

got got got got got got got got got got got got got got got got

gallantly revelled in their trills. They trilled the way

got got got got got got got got got got got got got got got got

one laughs weeps sighs curses kisses, then headfirst in a hailstorm of crystal notes, they all seemed to be looking for the bottom of the abyss where ecstasy and human sorrow lie.

Dialogues, musical repartees and duels. A defeated nightingale concedes with long passages of sobs. But a conspiracy of notes bursts out in the annoyed shade. The laughter slides down. Tumbling chords. Pause. In the conceited silence, another nightingale peeps out, sings in order to test the loyalty of distant echoes. He sings,

Getyu peepee hee Getyur sel fouto here

sings sings sings sings then falls into a trap. A mad carousel of voices…Cautiously, silence comes back to the surface. A long suspense swollen with wonder. And it was the nightingales who enforced that silence, as they conducted the chorale.

Now, a single nightingale. From his open beak,

agot agot agot agot agot agot

a fountain of notes-tears-stars spurted up, up, up, kisses that fell back down showering the second nightingale with gems.

tsotsotsotsotsotso

tsuddading got got

got got got

A hot longwinded stream of musical blood squirted out from this nightingale's heart and fell back down showering the third nightingale. The latter rushed into a whirl of pearls and furiously he began to choose, choose, discarding or hoarding the diamond trilling notes melodious gems and sorrowful rubies which were the second nightingale's drops of blood. And the stream of melody that spurt out from the first and all the melodious blood of the second made the other nightingales mad with artistic jealousy. All of them. Trying and trying again. To sing better. But they all preferred to improvise, and the one hundred, two hundred, three hundred nightingales cast wide nets of trills to cage in the leaves of the trees in their vast musical sweetness. Each net had thousands and thousands of hooks from which little fish of silver notes were hanging.

This is how the nightingales fished for flowers of light in the sea of leaves, and in their nets dripping with harmony they brought in all-enraptured hearts... Remembering...like seashells.

14

THE SCHOOL OF GOODNESS

In the meantime the Untameables, who had been tamed by the music of Goodness, were swimming in the lake. All of sudden Mirmofim stopped. He felt around for the bottom with his feet, and turning toward Kurotoplac and Curguss, who were swimming behind him, he said:

—Let's rest for a while. This swim is healthy. My heart feels so heavy in my chest. It's as if I didn't have elbows or fingernails anymore. A tenderness is welling up in me that wants to keep rising, rising. Look me in the eyes, Kurotoplac. Don't they seem different to you? Yours are as soft as a child's. In your eyes all the children you killed are smiling at you and forgiving you. I think I've finally learned how to smile. Look at Curguss! He's not the nasty old priest he used to be! What a cheerful and good-natured smile! Curguss, what do you think of my smile? You smile too. Let's all smile together. Let's see if you really know how to give a hug!

—I don't know how to, said Curguss humbly; you teach me!

Then Mazzapà the Negro spoke.

—It's been two hundred years, since my race practiced the coveted art of hugging a friend and holding him close to your heart! But tonight even the most difficult things seem natural.—How miserable you must be, all of you, not being able to hug one another because of your bloody armbands with their sharp studs.

—We're cursed! yelled Mirmofim. We'll never be able to hug anyone! We became brothers by wounding each other. We're doomed to express our affection by stabbing one another! But somehow, I feel that today we can hug each other.

—And about those studs, what do you plan to do with them? said Curguss.

—We'll try…very slowly…Come here Mazzapà! Listen to the musical love the nightingales and the liana harps are spreading about. Let's hug, Mazzapà! Let's all hug. With you, Mazzapà, and with you too, Curguss, and even you, Kurotoplac.

The Untameables hugged each other and were amazed that they were no longer hurting each other because the studs of their legbands, armbands, and frontlets bent easily in the grips of tenderness, like the tentacles of an octopus in the warm summer sea.

—Mazzapà! said Mirmofim, call Vokur and the other Negroes, so that I may kiss them all on the cheeks the way brothers kiss.

As the Negroes who had been summoned ran over and tried to crook their arms into an hug, the grand chorale of the forest doubled the pedal notes of its fleeting harmonies. The nightingales strained their ringing trills that begged for love. Each cry reached its apex, and you could feel that even higher another musical heaven was opening wide, hungry for a sweetness even more painful, higher, higher, towards the essence of absolute Goodness.

got got got got got
got got got got got got
got got got got got
got got got

At that moment Mirmofim threw his arms around all the Negro guards one by one. After the last kiss of the second cheek of the last Negro, he said:

—I finally know what goodness is!

The immense chorale immediately stopped. Stunned

got got geets

and overwhelmed by supreme wonder, the numberless musicians of the forest, fell silent and looked on blissfully.—Three minutes of silence. Then, the distinct voice of the great Paper Person rang out:

—I praise you all, Untameables, and you too, Negro guards, because you've discovered the great rhythm.

You are all worthy of entering the City! Come follow us, all of you!

There was a great sparkling flurry on the lake. The Untameables came out first, all streaming with light. Happy and docile as schoolchildren, they fell into a long line, and they headed down the path.

The path was shining even more brightly than before, and it could be seen curving around the lakeshore and then entering the thickets at the opposite point from which they had come.—The Negroes, who were slower and who were creatures of habit, gathered the chains, and with the muzzles clattering on their shoulders followed the Untameables. They felt they had the strength to walk for a long time, but they also realized without any concern that the essence of their bodies had in some way changed.

15

LIGHTING UP

—How strange! said Vokur to Mazzapà; I have the feeling that my legs are full of wind, and my head is floating up, up, up.

—It's only natural, answered Mazzapà; your head's a balloon anyway! But, you're right. I've never felt so light myself. My legs are as limp as wet cloth. Something, just now, passed through my memories, here, below my forehead: like a kind of lightening, a light in the dark. Who knows what it means! We Negroes are simple people, and we can never tell why something is or isn't...Tell me, Vokur: what purpose do these muzzles serve?

—I don't know. They're supposed to make a noise, like cowbells or buffalo bells, to let people know we're coming. If there's anybody waiting for us down there, they're certain to hear us, especially now that the birds have stopped singing. I don't miss their singing. I like silence and I like the dark. This darkness is great, and the damp feels good on my skin! I feel like the king of this Oasis!

The Untameables walked on in silence, but, every once in a while, they exchanged a few words that revealed how happy they were.

Overhead and all around them, thick shadows. But the glare of the path winding ahead of them became stronger and stronger.

—Mirmofim amused himself by weaving his steps in and out of the tangle created by the silver reflections and the long, black shadows. Every so often he'd kick a stone and it would dive into the darkness like a shooting golden ball.

He was walking at the head of the column and he often took Curguss by the hand because the priest couldn't see very well.

—Mirmofim, said Curguss, stopping suddenly; I feel like my head has fallen off my neck, and it feels like there's a fire here in my chest. Look.

Everyone stopped and gathered around the priest.

—This is a miracle! said Mirmofim, brushing his nose against his friend's chest.—Of course, I see, I see and I'm sure of it: your skin is transparent and there's a flame underneath. Two, in fact. They look like eyes of burning coal, and I can't see your face anymore. What the devil! It's turned to coal! By any chance have you changed your race, to show how much you like our Negro guards?...

In amazement everyone took a look for himself, and Curguss explained:

—It happened a little while ago, by the lake, when the nightingales began singing. I felt as if the music were burning my face. And it really was burning my face. Then I couldn't see anymore. Now, I see with my heart!...

Everyone was listening to Curguss in amazement, but not in fear. Peacefully, they all stood there in the dark, and they gently rocked back and forth as if their legs no longer touched the ground. They felt safe and calm like men glad to be hanging by the neck, feeling no pain, with their souls in better shape than ever.

Their limp legs began again to make indolent eel-slithering reflections and shadows.

—Just what I expected! said Mirmofim; I'm being changed into a lamp myself. Look! Look! Look!

His naked arms had become as luminescent as two mercury vapor tubes, and he raised them over his companions who had come rushing to him. Almost simultaneously, Kurotoplac's round head lit up with the white, studious, scientific light of a laboratory. Then, despite the feathery weakness in their legs, the Untameables picked up their pace. They had light of their own now, and the path could have just as well turned itself off. But it didn't. Instead, its brightness increased maddeningly, giving joy to the Untameables, and nurturing, nurturing them.

While the shadows thickened to the left and the right, where the trees hedged in their petrified battles, mysterious braziers of light kept exploding ahead of them, bundles of rays, whirling aureoles of gold, piercing duels of reflections. They all could sense that the path led to a great estuary of light that enclosed an even vaster sea of splendors beyond.[†]

---

† Only a Futurist sea could be more vast than the estuary which encloses it.—*Tr.*

16

THE CITY

Delighted with themselves, the Untameables walked on cheerfully cavorting like so many carefree children, while the Negroes milled around hesitantly, wavering between fear and hope, like enormous lumps of muscular coal. At times they would affectionately rub up against the Untameables, like happy mastiffs on a leash. Suddenly a great polished light-sound that looked like an ivory tube high in the leaves rang out. Its light formed a huge O of amazement in the dark silence.

The dazzling path climbed higher, but no one felt tired, since they all knew that soon they would finally learn how to see.

This was how the city appeared before them amidst the ancient shadows of the Oasis, lying wide open like a huge golden book. They all stopped in silence, over-whelmed by tenderness as if they had finally found their long lost mother.

The city appeared to lay on chaste and tranquil hills that lent to its varied silhouette, which bristled with light, the uninterrupted safe and heedless rhythm of a happy voyage.

The Untameables thought they might stop a while to better prepare themselves for the astonishing sensations lying ahead.

—Let's stop, said Curguss; we mustn't miss this sight. It demands all our respect and attention. Of course our senses are not sufficiently educated to take in all these new forms. I can see with the new eyes of my heart, but not very well, even though they're popping out of my chest.

—I can't see very well either, hardly at all, said Mirmofim, with these lighted arms of mine! Ah! if only their power to see were equal to their surgical skills! Instead, I feel like my arms are very nearsighted, tragically nearsighted. You'd need your whole body to light up, to live in that beautiful city of light.

He kept raising his right arm above him, as high as he could so as to explore, like a submarine in the dark-ness of the sea. At that point Kizmicà, a grim murderer with the head of an old and hungry wolf, began to tremble as if overcome by a fit of seizures.

No one had ever paid attention to him and to his

inexplicable silence. It was said that he had traveled all over the world murdering and robbing the rich, the poor and thieves like himself at random. What could be the matter with him? His mouth hung open, but not out of fierceness or hunger. Maybe he was just yawning. He must have been sleeping on his feet. But he suddenly gurgled like a drainpipe.

—How strange! My legs are lighting up!

Everybody congratulated him and his feet which were giving off light like electric lamps.

—What more could a vagabond like you hope for! Let's not waste any time! said Mirmofim; Time has come for us to go! Our friend Kizmicà will make out the writing on the path with his feet.

They had noticed in fact that as the path widened its light curiously broke down into phosphorescent writing. It was becoming a road lined with tombs. But what they had mistaken for tombs soon revealed their true nature. They were large open books, as tall as a man and luminous, but their light was gentle, almost human.

Their number increased. Then the first incandescent houses appeared. They were puzzling, fluid, built with unknown materials. None of the Untameables could tell what that substance really was. They came into a wide crooked and spacious street, with tall buildings of which some were lit more than others, and all varied in shape and proportion.

Those fluid buildings were made out of a powerful vapor that flowed incessantly upward creating the walls, changing the mass, the volume, the protrusions and the architectural form, so that in time they could take the shape of a cube, a sphere, an egg, a pyramid and an upside-down cone. The buildings had no windows, but movable cracks, wounds, mouths, eyes, funnels that opened and closed according to the ever-changing whims and will of the inhabitants.

But no matter how the forms varied, over all those houses of gleaming vapor there floated a point continuously adjusting its balance, a platform up above, a dominating and thinking terrace, or spire. The Untameables were so absorbed in the strangeness of those structures that it stopped them from noticing the crowd in the street. And an incredibly bizarre crowd it was.

There were many luminous Paper People, not unlike those they had already seen. There were also men who seemed almost normal, with whom the Untameables felt a distant kinship. Although brighter than they were, these men still had not achieved the brightness of lamps.

Occasionally, the Paper People would rush over to direct the flow, preventing the fastest ones from going into the narrow side streets, as if grave danger were waiting there. From the depths of those streets rose clouds of foul and acrid smoke.

Mirmofim, who had gotten into one of these streets, was forced to back out immediately, as if asphyxiated.

—I can tell you what that is, he told the curious Untameables. Down there, there are huge ovens and immense crucibles where the Paper People evidently burn their old things: burned cone-shaped robes, and shredded circumflex hats.

But a strange rumble attracted the attention of the Untameables.

The street sloped down through the vaporous buildings and grew more and more narrow like a funnel. Their curiosity was so overwhelming that none of them gave a thought to the possibility of danger, and so they arrived happily at the moving arch of a tunnel running through tall steel-smoke-dream girders. The ever-stranger rumbling was coming in gusts and it forewarned of the cavernous depths of endless underground vaults. The gluttonous abyss had accelerated their pace so much that it swallowed them up before they could enter.

Ambitious long-haired chimney peoples. Five Niagaras of fire. Staged naval battles. Daring leaps of gangways high over battleships shipwrecked in seas of mist. Outstretched fists of cranes fending off the assaults of rabid flames. Up high, the merry wheeling to and fro of tightrope dollies out of a circus. Rouge reflections on the fat cheeks of rivers. Broken evaporation shafts pimples of volcanoes. Blasts from furnaces. Sledgehammers pounding. Sparklers. Ray-needles injecting fire into the dusky flesh of sick shadows. Air vents panting like athletic trainers. Iron cages that detain monkeylike fires with red-violet asses. Voluptuous boulders of incandescent metal. They shower walls of relentless convents. Rebellious hawser peoples. Dripping, swirling, running, pirouetting, up and down. Vertically. Horizontally. Like a pendulum. Alternately like a mountain, a mouse, a turtle, like a feather.

Above, the Paper People shine unstainable, saints of this hell.

—Strange, said Mirmofim, who was walking at the head of the column, what we're breathing seems like smoke, but isn't. We can breathe in as much as we want. I don't think it bothers our lungs. Go ahead and take deep breaths. It seems like a vast human breath, dense, affectionate and clean.

The air was gray. The air darkened. They couldn't see anymore; they had to stop. But tongues of light flashed out, and Mirmofim once again led the column forward, into the sloping, narrow tunnel.

He walked holding up his two lighted arms, happy, with a scientific contentedness, his heart gripped by the foreboding of an inevitable truth.

—Ah! Ah! I never thought I'd be a candelabrum lit amid the faith of believers!

17

THE LIGHT AND PAPER WORKERS

They were in fact marching on in faith, like pilgrims in the catacombs, sure of an imminent apparition.

—It's the halos of the Saints! shouted Curguss who was able to cast a beam of golden light like a powerful bull's-eye lantern by holding his hands together over his flaming heart.

—Those aren't saints' halos that you see, said Mirmofim, they're the solid gold bellies of Buddha. Maybe we're in an Indian temple.

The air cleared, penetrated here and there by pale distant suns. Ten. Twenty. Thirty. The Untameables counted them, but those strange suns multiplied by the hundreds, and they continued to grow brighter. Finally they revealed what they really were. They were the spinning and shiny hubs of immense perpendicular wheels.

That wheel there on the right, it must be at least a hundred meters in diameter!

The vault soared on those fantastic perpendicular wheels with lyrical impetus and it formed an impassioned arch that rose rose disappearing in the darkness.

The air was tortured here and there by light and wholly rent by smoke, and as they continued to advance the Untameables understood that the wheels meshed into one other, at great speed.

Around each wheel the minute travail was seething with intricate clockwork made up of smaller wheels each of which was the height of a man and each of which carried a black flapping rag attached to its crank.

In silence the Untameables stopped, stricken with
r r r r r r r r r r r r r r r r r r r r r r r r r r r r r r r r r r r r r r r r r r r
amazement. Those rags seemed to be panting. They were
r r r r r r r r r r r r r r r r r r r r r r r r r r r r r r r r r r r r r r r r r r r
living beings. Flaccid, as if boneless, actually pulled
r r r r r r r r r r r r r r r r r r r r r r r r r r r r r r r r r r r r r r r r r r r
by the wheels, while in reality the energy to turn the
r r r r r r r r r r r r r r r r r r r r r r r r r r r r r r r r r r r r r r r r r r r
wheels came from them. Now and then, one of those limp and serpentine men would slow down his jerking movements. They could hear him gasp and groan from fatigue, while the wheels around him, still in gear, slowed down, and the giant perpendicular wheel re-

vealed its luminous silver sawtoothed edge, as it too lost speed. Just then a hissing cut through the blistering air.

—No slowing down! Back to work! Faster! faster! He who stops will be punished! Work or death! Speed or death!

The workers' yelps moans shouts sizzled in the darkness. They were countless. All of them were bent over their wheels. With growing astonishment the Untameables watched the precise figures that were flashing with luminous letters on the great board of the electric commutators.

10,000 right hands are in rotary action, 10,000 right feet, 10,000 grinding mouths.

But amid the hubbub of the workers you could make out some of the words.

—Yes, yes, work and speed. We'll take anything, but we're tired of turning the same wheel all the time!

—I want to diversify my work. Today I'll build a motor, tomorrow a sickle, the day after tomorrow a rifle!

—I'm tired of running a machine somebody else invented; I want to invent and build a whole new machine!

—Yes, yes, I want to invent things! We all want our own personal, inspired work. Everybody should create and build whatever he wants. Anything! Death to monotony!

—Long live imagination!

—Ah! if I could only use my left arm! I've been work-
ing for ten days with just my right arm, my left arm
feels like it'll be paralyzed before long!

—Down with menial work!

—Down with right-handed slavery!

—Long live the poetry of the body in freedom!

Gripped in anxiety, beneath the rumbling of the even
faster and more threatening perpendicular wheels, the
Untameables made their way amid the workers' outcries. Infernally.

They ran into a long column of black stooped men
who emerged three by three from the smoky depths of
the cavern swinging their right arms in time. Their left
arms were so feeble and limp that they appeared to be
maimed. These workers rocked on their right legs since
their nearly paralyzed left legs could barely support
them.

By the time the Untameables had left the last strag-
glers from the column behind, the air had changed. The
air was no longer rent by moaning and heavy panting,
but it was acrid and it reeked of the smells that rose in
whitish clouds from huge boiling caldrons.

—I know all about this, yelled out Kurotoplac. We're
in a paper mill.

Beneath the high domes shaped like endless chimneys the smoke of hundreds of caldrons rose lugubriously. Each caldron was as wide as a capital city's main
square and each was brightly encircled by the tracks
of the many trains that whistled, blazed and smoked

down there, in the depths of a giant railroad station. On the right above the first caldron the steel balustrade of the Brewing Observation Gallery glinted through the brimming smoke. A Paper Person appeared in his cone-shaped hat made of an upside-down book. Deadly white, a spectral hissing chalky white, the Paper Person hissed:

—All clear second train loaded with silk, velvet, purple dye, ostrich plumes!

Red signals rebounded, in that smoky subterranean immensity, like the flushed apoplectic faces of drunken and gluttonous demons.

A locomotive with a long silk trail of white horizontal steam rumbled and mooed and the train, a dromedary overloaded with cloth, skins, furs, and plumes, lurched forward as it encircled the entire caldron with its sinuous cars.

A crash of the first car's entire magnificent load as it is poured. The second disgorges an avalanche of ermine. The third car softens the material piled in the caldron with a shower of plumed fans, topping the whole with a flight of ostriches into a burning forest.

Like children drunk with wonder the Untameables ran toward the second caldron. It too was as wide a capital city's main square.

At the steel balustrade of the Brewing Observation Gallery, the great Chief of Paper-making appeared amid the billowing smoke. He too was a Paper Person, but whiter than the other. He was as blinding as a block of crystal struck by a hundred suns. He hissed:

—Send the fourth train loaded with all the Autumns, all the clouds of the sunsets and the dawns!...

The joyous lanterns winked simultaneously at their red stares.

The first car dumped into the cauldron a hundred red vintages, with whole lengths of autumnal vines crushed by thousands of grape-pickers' feet pumping as fast as racers in the most frenzied bicycle race.

The second car broke up into red tears, cutting out its veins and arteries like an enormous heart bulkily stuffed with all the hearts of grieving Madonnas and mothers widowed altogether of husband-son flesh and guts.

The fifth car inundated the caldron and all the caves around it near and far with a profusion of rose carmine ruby decayed light heavy ecstatic prophetic drunken inebriating gilded mad and melancholy clouds.

With the sole intent of conquering every black night, those ruffled clouds overran everything, they tinged everything, they rushed everywhere.

The great Chief of Paper-making hissed again:

—Call the fog train!

Soapily slipping without a sound on the gleaming tracks, the fog train arrived like a great nacreous ribbon, and it emptied its fluid cars permeating everything with gray.

Everyone was suddenly blinded.

—Damn it...where are you? shouted Mirmofim. All

the Untameables here! This is London fog. It's as if I were still there with my scalpel in hand not knowing what to do like the time that awful London fog poured into the hospital and suddenly hid the edges of the wound I was operating on. I was dazed and I thought I was a lightning-surgeon magically suspended over the tempestuous rift that they call the English Channel. Below me the foggy wound seemed as long as this cauldron.

In the meantime a vast rustling and wailing sound began to grow, similar to that of the Oasis, but even more so like the sound of an uprising.

As the Untameables accelerated their pace they would have liked to ask somebody about all this; but all the human beings had disappeared, and they met only the Paper People who slipped away in the whirl of their translucent cone-shaped robes.

—As much as everything might seem new to us in this strange city, said Mirmofim, I have the feeling that this rhythm of life is not the usual rhythm of the city.

—Of course...said Curguss, I have the same feeling that something unusual is happening. These Paper People we're running into are a little too worried. In any case it's odd that they're ignoring us!

—I'm not so sure, said Mazzapà. They despise us because we're just peons, and here they're all lords, princes, and kings!

18

THE UPRISING

But Mirmofim was right, and the Untameables realized it when they came into a large square, closed in on three sides by tall fluid buildings made incandescent by the pressure of a growing crowd of Paper People and semi-luminous men. They did not shout nor did they speak, but they all hissed like thousands of winter winds in thousands of different keyholes.

All at once, the crowd fell silent and the semi-luminous men raised their heads. On the oscillating vaporous pediment of one of the buildings there appeared a strange flared megaphone that seemed to be made of transparent metal.

A gigantic tongue made of fire throbbed inside of it. The Untameables understood: a Great Paper Person was lying flat on the roof, in order to speak horizontally with his body lit up, similar to an eloquent flame-tongue.

—Paper People! he began; you who have already reached the state of luminous grace, and you, semi-luminous Men, who will certainly achieve the state of luminous grace, I plead with you to support the cause of the oppressed River People! I am not a River Person, but I love the River People and I defend their sacrosanct right to flow freely and to rest and dilute in the Lake of Poetry!

The crowd wove together thousands of angry hisses.

—This hissing, said Kurotoplac, is applause! Apparently the Paper Person who's speaking is a Paper revolutionary. Let's hear what he has to say.

—The River People, the Paper Person began again from the roof of the building with his horizontal tongue of fire,—the River People are no longer the scattered, rejected and irresponsible people they once were. They've united to form a single river, and as such they no longer want to subject themselves to the embankments where they laboriously turn the great wheels of the illuminating motors. They want their river to flow freely through the Oasis, and to mix with the waters of the great Lake of Poetry, for therein lies the peace that they have demanded for so many years. But the privileged Paper People who rule us are opposed to their freedom. This is an abuse of power! It is an injustice! The former government, who better understood the times, had conceded a great deal to the River People, and for this reason a bed leading from the city was dug to divert the course of the river toward the Lake of Poetry. About thirty meters from here, their ancient hope to flow unrestricted is held captive by the impenetrable Cardboard Dam.

—The Cardboard Dam is choking the arteries of the world! Put aside your fear. Get ready! The hour is coming when you will have to launch an attack on the great Cardboard Dam!

There was shrieking, howling, shouting!

—Rain! Rain! Rain!

It wasn't really raining. Just a few drops. But the fear of rain shook the city. Five Paper People were extinguished. Others flickered. A great Paper Person animated by a blue flame made his way through the crowd, which was all patches of light and shadow. He was followed by eleven blue Paper People, who were smaller and not as brightly lit. Marching in step, they formed an orderly circle around the great Paper Person. Then, each made a half right turn, and bent over the cone-shaped robe of his neighbor. They were all ready to take dictation with their elongated blue hands, which were made even longer by blue brushes.

The rain poured down, poured down, extinguishing the city. The crowd had disappeared. Only the Untameables had remained to watch the strange ritual. Like a diamond set against other diamonds, the great Paper Person said:

—Rain of Time and Tedium, you will not conquer

the city! My song is enough to put you to flight. I challenge you! I challenge you! I challenge you! Cast down your water-boredom and I will hurl light into the sky! Cast down your darkness rot and terror, and I'll send up joy, blue joy!

And didn't the struggle of those living diamonds of tenacious light rage against the murky offensive of destructive Rain for a long time!

The Untameables looked on with fascination as the eleven Paper People decorated each other's cone-shaped robes with blue writing, while the great Paper Person, who was getting bluer and more dazzling, dictated:

—The reign of Light is at hand! Light will triumph! With speed, in speed, from speed Light will burst forward. Speedlight! Speedlight! The whole world hopes for Light. We are real Light. Diamond! Diamond! I am the Diamond poet!

From the zenith, there was an abrupt avalanche of light. A hundred thousand thousand Paper People sprang forward together and lit up. The instantaneous living illumination formed a column. Caught up in the current, the Untameables followed. A voice cried out:

—Let's go to the River!

Other Paper People appeared on the roofs of the vapor buildings which were lighting up again. They were horizontal with their body-tongues lit up in the acoustic cone of their robes. Motionless as if they were about to speak. They were all different sizes. Some very young, children. Others adults. Others were very old.

The flowing crowd came to a halt. The road must have been blocked. The Untameables began to nose around. They noticed that lying on the ground around each building there were two or three of those same monumental books which had amazed them when they first entered the city. A few steps from Mirmofim, one of them suddenly burst open, with a jerky flourish of colored pages. The liveliest of the pages tears itself from the book with a rapid whirl, forms a cone, pastes itself shut, stands up with its point on top. Just then, a light buds inside and as it grows it becomes redder and more fiery.

Thus was born a Paper Person. A written thought magically transformed into action-life. Mirmofim, who became more and more passionately caught up in the mysteries of the city, called to the other Untameables:

Look! he said; Look at the gray vapor spreading from this Paper Person's flaming body, and compare it to the walls of the buildings. I'm convinced that every Paper Person builds his own vapor-light house with the same gas that his own fiery body gives off. These big books lying here are the cradles, the beds and the graves of the Paper People.

19

CRADLES, BEDS AND GRAVES

As he spoke amid the mob of Untameables, another book opened suddenly at their feet, like a trapdoor, and it gave them a terrible fright. Besides the jagged ends of the many self-torn pages that had been changed into mobile life, there was just one page.

The page was flapping.

—Kizmicà, go closer, go closer with those luminous feet of yours, and read that page!

Kizmicà, who like the rest of the Untameables obeyed the surgeon blindly, rushed forward, and said:

—I've traveled all around the world and I know every language. Putting them all together, I should be able to figure out this language that I've never seen before.

Then, pointing his luminous feet at the page, he began to read.

—At the top of the page, which must have been the last page of the book, I can see the words: "The Social Contract by Jean Jacques Rousseau"....In the center of the page, I see the words: THE END.

The Untameables could not contain their scientific curiosity. They were intent on reading all of those marvelous books lying on the ground. Kizmicà jumped forward, quick to illuminate the flapping pages with his luminous legs, and he deciphered out loud as he conferred with Mirmofim. In this manner they determined that the books most torn, damaged and with practically no pages left had the most powerful spiritual life. The others, still closed, unused and still full of pages, proved to be sterile or embittered, and in any case incapable at the moment of transforming their pages into living Paper People. One of the most worn books fell open to reveal a splendid iridescent blue page, on which Kizmicà could read the word: MAZZINI.†

In the meantime the crowd of Paper People and semiluminous men continued to riot, trying desperately to push their way through the street and reach the embankment of the river, which was gurgling and roaring.

No one in the crowd paid any attention to the Untameables who were anxiously nosing around like

†   Giuseppe Mazzini (1805-72), Italian patriot and political thinker of the *Risorgimento* (the Italian unification movement).

woodworms in a queer library of books which lay flat on the ground.—There were the great books of Spinoza, Pascal, Machiavelli, Vico, Nietzsche, Kant, Marx. Gawking like a bunch of yokels, the Untameables stopped before the largest and most luminous of the books. It opened incessantly, and its pages, as if dank with comic blood, fluttered the same way flags twirl themselves into the shape of a cone.

The Paper Person who was thus formed darted away with incredible speed, and he immediately climbed up the steps of the incandescent buildings and perched himself imperiously on one of the terraces. In just a few seconds, that potent book gave birth to 22 Paper People. They weren't ordinary Paper People. The cone of their robes had the splendor of a cone-shaped diamond.—For a second, they just stood there the way Paper People usually did; then, turning upside down, they presented the round orifice of their bodies to the stars. Thus transformed into projectors, they printed radiant adamantine words in freedom in the sky.

Those brilliant shafts of light traveled searching the night sky, and they erased the ancient constellations, and new stars blossomed, and they wrote, they wrote with mad letters of light, frightening thoughts of mysterious beauty.

20

TOWARD FUTURISM

With their faces turned upward, Mirmofim and all the other Untameables strained to read that celestial writing. They were driven by unbearable curiosity. They thought of everything they could.

Suddenly they seemed to have found a way, and it was Mazzapà who came up with it:

—Yes, that's it...One on top of the other...Let's climb up there...At the bottom, we need a good solid base. The 20 strongest among us, with their arms folded. Another 18 on top of them. On those 18, 16 more. And so on, higher and higher.

The Untameables climbed and wove together like a tower of Babel and the pyramid was raised. Everybody helped, sure of success. The craving to understand what was written in the sky gripped every heart. Up they went, higher and higher. And although the colossal Negroes, the most dull-witted and brawniest among them, had the task of supporting the pyramidal tower at its base, they didn't moan at all.—Mazzapà, who bore a great part of the weight on his giant caryatid shoulders, roared out:

—Send Mirmofim the surgeon to the top of our pyramidal tower! He's the most clairvoyant and the most daring of us all!

Mirmofim, the last one left, climbed up. When he was at the summit of the swaying but balanced human tower, he stuck out his chest and took a deep breath, proud and happy to be as high as the highest incandescent vaporous building.

The shafts of light projected into the sky by the upside-down Paper People had multiplied, crisscrossing each other. The sky was a forest of searchlights writing their words of cutting fire. To the right and left, other searchlights, immense plows and rakes of light tilled the endless black plains of the sky.

Mirmofim raised his luminous arms, and he gazed, he gazed, he gazed, upward, upward. But he couldn't make anything out. He felt dull-witted, heavy, and he let himself tumble down, grappling the human corners of the tower which fell apart collapsing into sobs of pain and cruel defeat. But Kizmicà led all the Untameables back to the great book that continued to give birth to adamantine Paper People.

They all hunched over the luminous splendor of the flapping pages, like yokels visiting the deck of a transatlantic liner who bend over to peer through the glowing portholes at the hot fury of the engines.

In fact the great book was not only a gaping and inexhaustible womb, but also a tireless engine of the sailing city of Thought.

Kizmicà had been standing upright for five minutes, with his head bowed, carefully watching his luminous legs as they lit up the birth of the fluttering pages with rosy reflections. They twirled away so fast that no one could read them.

—I read one! I read one! he shouted. I read these words:

"THE FUTURIST MANIFESTOS. MARINETTI"

Mirmofim jumped up as if struck by decisive inspiration:

—Friends! Friends! Listen to me closely! All those Paper People and semi-luminous men who are rioting, they need a leader! They're all crying out for one, but they can't find him. They want to be able to recognize him with the naked eye. They want to taste him first like a piece of meat well-done. What idiots! The great book of Futurism teaches us to make everything up, even God! We've got to make up a leader for that crowd. I am that leader! Come with me!

They all rushed after Mirmofim, who dug through the crowd and injected it with the energy of the Untameables as he ran. The luminous crowd made way, amazed that an unknown dark force could rip it apart.— The immense crowd of living lamps was soon dominated and led by that throng of swift black coals. Those lamps had forgotten their strength, perhaps because they were so used to their own steady light. Perhaps those blind coals, for the very reason that they were blind, possessed an unmitigated creative vision.

21

THE RIVER PEOPLE

The crowd followed Mirmofim and the Untameables. Accustomed as they were to abusing their bodies, they broke through the obstacles made of condensed vapor and cardboard. The Untameables did not share the precious fragility of the Paper People. They bloodied themselves in order to break through more easily. Getting bloody, wasn't that their natural way of living, loving and thinking?

The revolutionary lamp people and the semi-luminous men rushed after the dark Untameables. They were still in the lead. Forward! Wreck everything! God! what pushing and shoving! Who would dare speak of caution? No chance! There's only one road! Follow your nose, all the way, head first! Madly breaking through breaking through going running running…Here are the parapets that plunge down into the river!

The thundering river flowed rapidly, with a clamorous roar made up of millions of interwoven roars.—That formidable current contained curses solidified in the form of knotted ropes, teardrops in the form of women, sobs in the form of tubercular babies, vendettas in the form of elephant teeth, hatred in the form of steel saws, long threats-whips, curses-daggers, kisses-bites, throttling embraces, bilious smiles, slobber of winter dawns, jaundice of anarchical twilight, revolutionary marching taverns, a hundred thousand red bottles talking and gesticulating, the backs of a billion servants who turn into ferocious wheels from bending over, all the wicked bloody deeds of the poor who have become living beings without shirts on their backs, with red belly buttons the seal of levy-inflicted death.

That river blended all of life under the frazzled coiffure of unsatisfied desires that played about in heaven.—Up high, on the other bank, the tall incandescent vapor buildings bore the Great Paper Governors like dominating statues on their facades and terraces.

Above them, the sky was a tangled forest of bright shafts that were writing writing from the bottom to the top on the arching vault of the night, all the way up to the zenith.

Then, as if it could feel the pressure of the revolu-

tionary Paper People and the Untameables who v
crowding the embankment, the Great River upset the
rhythm of its flowing water it rippled with yelling mouths
and frantically clapping hands and bristling hair so as
to cheer its liberators.

ey ey ey ey ey ey ey
aaaaaaaaa   uuuuuuuuu
rrrrrrrrrr   vvvvvvvvvv
eeeeeeeeeeeeeeeeeeee

The hurricane of applause lasted an hour. Then
Mirmofim, who strutted with great seriousness puffing
out his chest and throwing his head back, spoke as a
recognized leader:

—I salute you, great River People. I have led this
crowd of revolutionary Paper People and semi-luminous men to you to meet you, to admire you and to help
you in the final battle. I come from the great Lake of
Poetry!

A wild cheer leaped forth from the river, and billions of river mouths were overwrought with joy to greet
the man from the Lake. All of those mouths shouted
together:

—To the Lake! To the Lake! To the Lake!

Mirmofim, with his arms stretched out horizontally,
went on:

—You are right to shout like this. You must sense
the divine sweetness contained in the Lake of Poetry.
In the Lake, all humiliation, all suffering, all crying,

...ally be extinguished. The great Paper
...you in chains in their city have ceased
...have toiled for too long under their
..., running the illuminating wheels, bent
... without ever being able to raise your heads
to revel in the spirit of the sky. Now those dogs despise
you, since you don't know how to look at anything except the ground and your footprints. I'll teach you to
nimbilize your necks and see the sky!

Mirmofim was interrupted by a long long long hiss,
sinuous and jagged, a saw or choking uvula.

The hissing came from the tall incandescent vapor
buildings on the other side of the river. Two glowing
Paper People appeared on the highest terrace. A name
ran from mouth to mouth, through the silent crowd gathered at the embankment.

—*Notnor, Notnor, Notnor…*

It was the hiss of Notnor, who was speaking: Notnor,
one of the absolute rulers.

In the pause of total silence, Notnor spoke:

—Nooo! Nooo! Nooooo! The River People will continue to obey!…They are brute force, quantity. Only
we can command; we: who are quality!

—That's untrue! shouted Mirmofim. Everything that
used to be is wrong, because it used to be. Everything
that has not been is right, because it has not been! It
will be! Quality has been! We're going to do away with
it! Quantity has never ruled! It shall rule! We will it!

This sibylline speech agitated the crowd of revolutionary Paper People and semi-luminous men at the embankment. Even the River People didn't understand. Confusion, uneasiness.

Wavering. Yes. No. Why? Is it me or him, the idiot? Murmuring of a skeptical sea. A rain of doubt on men's souls.

Mazzapà, who was holding Mirmofim up in his athletic arms so that he could better dominate the crowd, said:

—Speak clearly. I didn't understand a word you said. Explain yourself better. If you don't, your adoring crowd will do you in.

The shaky indecision of the crowd played into the hands of the Paper Governors, and so the second Paper Person let his soft voice drip down from the other bank curled with treachery.

—I am Yessir, and I have governed your city for many years. You all know me, even you River People. I never said *No!* to your demands for freedom. I was always your friend and when you asked to flow unhindered to the Lake of Poetry, I answered *Yes!*…Now, in the name of the new government, I still say *Yes!* So rest assured: you will go to the Lake of Poetry. The bed in which you will flow has already been excavated. Don't forget that this wholesome bed was dug at my orders!

A hurricane of joyous hissing cheered his generous speech. It seemed to everybody, the revolutionary Paper People, the semi-luminous men, and the River People alike, that the ancient issue of flowing freely to the Lake of Poetry had been miraculously resolved, thanks to the paternal goodwill of the governors.

A solemn heavy silence. Yessir went on:

—Yes, you shall go to the Lake of Poetry. Yes! Not everyone, however! Some of you will have to continue the great work that is so necessary to the city!

Mirmofim instantaneously sensed Yessir's mistake and sprang forward:

—Liar! Impostor! Shyster! You conceal betrayal! River People, don't listen to Yessir anymore! The time to revolt is upon us! revolutionary Paper People, and you, my brother Untameables, follow me! Let's smash down the great Cardboard Dam of condensed vapor that stops the river from flowing through the forest to the Lake of Poetry! That dam won't hold for long! It's old, rotten! It won't hold. Come on!

—No! No! Wait! a revolutionary Paper Person yelled at Mirmofim.

He was very popular and respected for his great honesty and wisdom. Well…was his name. Everyone quieted down to listen to Well….

—Wait! he said. This is a critical moment. Before deciding anything, we must examine the condition of the dam and determine whether or not the free course of the river, which we all rightfully call for, will also, as I fear, sweep us, the indispensable Lamps, away, and with us the illuminating spirit that must guide the river to the great Lake of Poetry. Let's see if there is, by chance, a way of reconciling the right to flow freely with the continuity of the illuminating Spirit. For your sake, for ours, for everyone's, I hope that the River People's desire will be fulfilled and that they will finally flow toward the Lake of Poetry, while they continue to supply light to the city. I am not a conservative, as you all know. I am an old revolutionary, and it pains me to say to you: Wait!, since between my suffering and all of your suffering there is no patience left. But revolutionary wisdom and the experimental art of violence force me to pronounce these lacerating words: Wait! Reflect! We shall decide tomorrow!

—No! No! No! cried Mirmofim. The great Tomorrow is here in our hands! Death to the City! Death to the illuminating Spirit! Down with Yessir! Down with Notnor! Down with Well...! Let's destroy the dam! To the Lake! To the Lake! To the Lake! To the Lake!

Shouting and swelling globulously, the crowd threw itself behind Mirmofim, who was held high on Mazzapà's shoulders as if he were on top of a rock, waving his phosphorescent arms around like a fisherman who had just gutted some rotting whales.

22

THE CARDBOARD DAM

As they rioted between the embankments, the River People all turned upside-down, so that their river would reverse its course and head straight for the Cardboard Dam. When the Untameables reached the towering gates of the dam with its 200 bolts, Mirmofim and Mazzapà climbed up on the bars and began to hack at the wall of reinforced cardboard with their axes. The revolutionary Paper People and the semi-luminous men on one side, and the River People on the other, cheered the destructors with wild cries:

—Smash it! Smash it! Smash it! Break through! Rip it apart! Rip it apart!

Mirmofim labored at that tough surgical operation with his two luminous arms, finally content at being able to open a belly worthy of him. The mass of furious River People pushed against the dam with all their teeth and bristling hair in order to screech and to file away at the tenacious surface, and the dam swelled up like a belly under Mirmofim's surgical hand.

Kurotoplac, who was drilling, hanging on to another of the dam's gates, shouted:

—Watch out! The center is cracking! This gate's giving way! Watch out! It's giving way!

He had just enough time to tumble down and to get back on top of the embankment.

BIDIBANG BANG BANG CRAAAACK

sssssssssssssssssssss

rrrrrrrrrr zzzzzzzz sssssssss rrrrrrrrrr

u u u u u u u u u u u u u u u u u

The gate shot straight open the way a madman shoots off his thoughts.

Thirty thousand River People, towering waves, coils, assaults of water, were squirted horizontally across the city through that opening.

Tum Tum Turuzeey

FROOON BOOAAM FROOON BOOAAM

The second gate burst open, while Mirmofim was yelling to the embankment:

—Get out of here! Get out of here! Follow me!…Up the hill on the right!…We must get to the high ground of the city! It won't be long before the lower neighborhoods are all flooded! Quick! Get out of here!

A thundering crash, whining shrills. F
wounded beasts. Bombardment of echoes,
pulent slamming. The dam fired, pounded ma
gunned. Down down go the River People, filling up the
squares and streets...

ᵹᵹ
ᵹᵹ

Here's a cascade of bubbling and screeching River
People plunging down from the terrace up there into
the ditch. It's already full to the brim. It overflows. As
two old incandescent vapor buildings are surrounded
by the flow, the frenzied thrust of that liquid crowd
makes them tremble, and they totter and sag as if about
to fall apart.

The whole city appears to be flooded by the blue
River People, who were slipping their stirring currents
everywhere as they turned blue the way the sea turns
blue in a gulf thick with vegetation. But the younger
white incandescent vapor buildings rocked gracefully
and solemnly, without crumbling. Some of them, which
had already been sheared at the base by the blue
current's immense razors, floated majestically on the
surface. From the trembling profile of the luminous
buildings, the impassive Futurist Paper People reigned
on high, as they intensified their function as immortal
lamps.

Almost indifferent to the River People's great blue

ᵹᵹ

revolution, they continued to beam up at the sky, with

ggggggggggggggggggggggggggggggggggggggggggggggggggg
the horizontal cones of their robes, their elongated light-

ggggggggggggggggggggggggggggggggggggggggggggggggggg
chalk fingers writing imperious words in freedom.

In the meantime, Mirmofim ran as fast as he could with the Untameables to high ground as they sought to flee the wild current of River People, who plundered everything in the path of their devastating rolling and tempestuous fury. Mirmofim's body seemed to have lost all human weight. Around him, along with him, everything was bouncing sliding and running. His mouth had been opened wide by the frightened thrust of his heart which was just ahead of him.

—The path! The path! Where's the path? Quick! We must find the path again, before the River People's blue current gets here!

—There it is! There it is! shouted Kizmicà with his lighted feet.

And Mirmofim rushed into the Oasis waving his luminous arms. The Untameables were right behind him, running in a frenzy, bumping into trees, and tumbling down. The vaguely phosphorescent path guided them. But Kizmicà's feet were slowly dimming. They couldn't see the path anymore. They stopped. They had to catch their breath. Curguss said:

—We mustn't stop! If we stop, we're lost! It won't be long before we'll hear the River People's sinister roar again.

Their hearts beat loudly in the silence of the forest, like the powerful rhythmic mournful bubbling of a saucepan. They panted, laboriously, sitting on the ground, straining to recognize the regal columns of camerus, the stingy secrecy of the carobs, the bold swordsmanship of the agaves, and the barbaric pranks of the cactus.

The darkness was massive. But it cracked. A light clear streak then two light blue streaks, and the tragic roaring could be heard again. Just then, the depths of the Oasis were filled with a peaceful blue light.

—Let's get out of here! cried Mirmofim.

They rushed into the darkness, following their noses, like dogs trying to retrace their own footsteps. They couldn't find them. The path was lost forever. In the face of this tremendous bellowing blue invasion, they could do nothing but flee for their lives.

To the right, to the left, up above, the undulating of

gggggggggggggggggggggggggggggggggggggggggggggggggggg
the leaves, still dreamy from their nocturnal delights,

gggggggggggggggggggggggggggggggggggggggggggggggggggg
became stiff and as they metallized they sizzled like

gggggggggggggggggggggggggggggggggggggggggggggggggggg
they would in a crucible. The vegetal vault under which they were running was now a bronze vault. Behind them they could feel the quivering of the River People's blue invasion, and in front of them, in the distance, they could see the first red stabs of the sun. To the right and

to the left, the trees creaked as they grew hard, vibrating like copper statues in an earthquake.

But it became even more frightening, since the vegetation of the Oasis, which grew thicker and thicker, accelerated its metallization with brutal contortions and fannings of its leaves.

—Keep your heads down! Keep your heads down! Run with your heads down! Kurotoplac kept shouting.

The branches that had collapsed, exhausted with weakness, sprung up and became stiff resonant ceilings of vibrating metal. The angry grass stabbed the Untameables' running legs. The great liana harps leapt up, tightening themselves like metallic strings stretched by the movement of invisible aerial pegs.

The solar furnace opened ahead of the Untameables at the end of the Oasis. It was the target of their mad dash. Twice, Mirmofim avoided the rabid lashes of a stiff branch. But the third branch struck him full on, and he collapsed to the ground.

He got up bleeding. Other Untameables tumbled down, after being whipped by the bronze rods of the Oasis that growled and taunted them.

—Let's get out! Out! yelled Curguss. Damned Oasis!…

The Oasis hated them, and it was intent on flogging them to death. The Untameables could sense that the moment of truth had arrived. The leaves whirled about overhead, as if caught in a waterspout. First they'd loom above the fugitives, then pretend to be distracted, then down, straight down, onto their backs.

With monkey jumps and lightening eel-ings, the cunning Untameables slipped away on the cruel wind of one last bronze lash. They all fell and sank into the burning sand. They were exhausted. They raised their heads and looked at the austere sun which was poised high above them like an ax. They smiled at it, the way you smile at the kind, redeeming mouth of your mother.

23

THE DEATH OF MAZZAPÀ

Mirmofim was the first to come to. His eyes bulged from their sockets, swollen with cruelty and spite, and when he saw his fellow Untameables and the great bodies of the Negro soldiers lying in the sand, he grumbled:

—At least we could have left our filthy Negro guards down there!

Mazzapà, who was lying on his back without moving, said:

—Don't start again, you damned surgeon!

Without answering, Mirmofim threw himself on Mazzapà's neck and began choking him, choking him with all the strength of his surgical fingers.

The Negro was very strong, but he was tired and he

was pinned down. He tried to break free by twice heaving himself up from the waist. But the surgeon, with concentrated malicious nervous effort, was digging out Mazzapà's belly with his knees. While his hands knotted Mazzapà's throat. Severely. The tired faces of the Untameables and the Negro soldiers turned toward them, but they didn't believe that this squabble could be fatal, and they laughed. Not one of them got up, being that they were too tired to be interested in this battle.

The towering bronze wall of the Oasis seemed to have passed invisibly into the surgeon's hands. Mazzapà's mouth became round. Out came his tongue, red like a wounded lizard, and it immediately disappeared, while his white yellowish, fierce, sweet eyes rolled in death. The surgeon stood up, and stretching his arms, he said:

—Not bad! I can still perform an operation.

They understood all around what had happened and rushed toward Mazzapà's corpse. Vokur postponed his howls of rage, and he called his comrades who were heartened in their bones and their muscles by their reborn hate. They immediately took charge of the Untameables, who were still shaky on their feet, dumfounded, brutalized by that unexpected death. The Negro soldiers chained the Untameables, and, using their bayonets and cursing, they ordered them into a column under the Sun which was reestablishing its empire of molten lead as it conquered the zenith.

Chained at the wrists, Mirmofim walked at the head

of the column, and he spat now and then at Vokur who kept sticking him in the buttocks.

—Tomorrow, Mirmofim kept saying, you lousy Negroes will be in chains, instead of us. I'm glad I killed Mazzapà. Tomorrow I'll disembowel you, Vokur!

Once they had passed the Dune of Camels, the Untameables were not surprised when they saw the Paper People standing there in the yellow cones of their robes, which were lined with writing, and the circumflex books upside-down on their heads. Dragging their feet, they went down into the pit, while the Negro soldiers headed toward the Paper People.

Like obedient mastiffs, the Negro soldiers offered their weary spherical heads to the Paper People, who methodically and unhurriedly clamped new muzzles on them. The locks could be heard creaking shut over their pug-nosed faces.

In the meantime, the Untameables had lain down, heaped up on top of one another, in the center of the pit.

When the Paper People left slipping across the dunes toward the reddish bronze Oasis in the distance, Vokur sat down tired in the sand, with his muzzle. Then, remembering his companion Mazzapà and the way he used to cry out under the noon sun, with the same rough and crude voice, he said:

—I'm thirsty, Mazzapà!

No one answered.

Then he flopped down on his back, and he fell asleep, with his mouth hanging open under the sparkling steel muzzle.

From up high, the sun drenched him, paternally, with molten lead.

24

ART

But the Untameables weren't sleeping. They were boiling. Mirmofim sprang forward and shouted:

—There it is! There! There! Inside of me I can see everything that happened last night in the Oasis and on the shores of the lake!

They all stood up and there was a commotion.

—What do you see? Tell us! Tell us! Tell us what you see!

—Ah! finally, finally my brain is opening up!

Vokur had woken up. He thought the Untameables were rebelling, and he reached for his rifle. He found two: his and Mazzapà's. He grabbed one with his right hand, the other with his left hand, and he went down into the pit.

The Untameables were crowded intently around Mirmofim, who was telling his story with his head bowed down:

—We are led into the dark Oasis by a phosphorescent path that sways between the towering trees…

Reassured, Vokur crouched down in the sand near the edge of the pit. He held the bayonets of two rifles crossed in his hands. Since his hands were trembling, the bayonets clinked together.

—A soft sweetness rains down from the leaves…the path becomes more and more luminous…

The clinking of the bayonets kept time with Mirmofim's voice and his grinding teeth.

Thus, the superhuman fresh-winged Distraction of Art, stronger than the raw dissonance of Sun and Blood, finally effected the metamorphosis of the Untameables.

THE END

APPENDIX

Two African Books on Marinetti[†]
(*La Nazione di Trieste*, August 18, 1922)

The creator of Futurism is an African. Whoever wants to forget it will be reminded by him from time to time. Born in Egypt; Sudanese nurse; a wild childhood before an education in Paris as a youth. He has a lot of Africa in his blood; and in his wanderings—sometimes he is alone, sometimes he is at the head of a pack of poets, painters, melomaniacs, bizarre artists—there is a sort of nomadic tent-dweller instinct, like that of a tribal chieftain.

It was Nietzsche who first turned toward Africa to ask for a sun-crazed art, an art disinfected and purified by the burning sun. He had an intuition of the original link between African barbarism and Mediterranean civilization, the same link that would give a new direction to much of scientific research only a few years later. He was one of the few Europeans who thought of Africa in its intensity, in other words as a land where one could reach the maximum, the strongest of feelings. Marinetti, who was born in Africa, never let go of this impression. His *Mafarka il futurista* [*Mafarka the Futurist*], a most

[†] Did he perhaps mean *by Marinetti*?

unusual book, finds in the African atmosphere a violence of color and breath that the author could never
have imagined in any other part of the world. In other
books that he wrote during the war, the impetus and
the savage furor of certain war episodes spontaneously
engaged African tonalities of combustion, fierceness,
Negro merriment. They were completely new literary
expressions, and more significant for us than the entire
theoretical construction of Futurism. Marinetti possesses the African sensibility to the same extent that
an English Lake poet possesses the misty ambience of
the lakes, or a Carduccian poet[†] possesses the Italian
landscape, with its rivers, poplar trees, hills, cypress
trees, roads, cicadas.

Now he has published two new books where his
imagination has been set free once again in the implacable fiery African air. One of the two books belongs to
the dramatic genre, and it is already famous for the
applause it has received in many cities: it is the play, *Il
tamburo di fuoco* [*The Fire-Drum*]. It has been written
about even in this newspaper, and no doubt it will be
talked about again when it will be performed in one of
our theaters. Critics found this work no different from
many other plays that can be said to have a passeist-
structure; but I find it rather different from many oth-

[†] An imitator of the Italian poet, Giosuè Carducci (1835-1907).

ers because of its blowing, hot gusts of poetry, each one impetuous and spontaneous, born in an incontestably sincere sympathy between artist and the mysterious country of adventure where man receives his law from the battle with elephants and reptiles, with the sands and mirages, with the feverish forests and calcifying deserts. Those who read only the reviews will never have any idea of *Il tamburo di fuoco*; you must read the play to feel how this poet has ignited—it is better to read it than to see it at the theater, burdened by mechanical expedients.

It is hard to say if the other book, *The Untameables*, is a novel, a poem, an allegory, a parable, and the poet himself is uncertain as to the denomination that it ought to be assigned: it seems to me that it has certain affinities—of which the author may be unaware—with the imagination and projection in some of Wells' books. The Negro soldiers, with their mastiff heads closed up in the steel muzzles, belong to the progeny of monsters that the English writer conceived in order to characterize brute barbarism; and to the world of Wells also pertain the "Paper People," animated and humanized pages of books who govern and discipline the savage life, and the "River People," liquid masses of people, who, yearning for freedom and poetry, burst into the monstrous cities where they had been forced to work like slaves. But Wells, in his social allegories and his prophetic theorems, has the meticulous clearness of the thinker and distributor of the functions of his own thought; whereas Marinetti, the volcanic spirit, dragged by his own lyricism or dwelling on the fascinating power of his own sensations, does not arrive at a balance of all the lights in the social vision he would perhaps like to express in his strange book. There is undoubtedly a great disproportion between the first part which is powerful, distinctive, shaped with great fire, and awesome, and the second part which is blurry and fleeting, seemingly jotted down in a hurry, as if by someone impatient to finish the book.

In the first part—furnace air, heavy and implacable light, leaden materiality, brute cruelty, a perception of a border between man and beast, between the extreme breathable air and the air where one can no longer breath—Marinetti conveys the meaning of Africa with imaginative force, with clear figures of speech and unthought-of comparisons that take possession of us through a sensation held in place by new and domineering words. It is a wholly compacted palette of ochre, of burnt earth, of blinding white lead, without mitigation. Later, the imagination moves, sweeps, becomes bluish in the music of a tropical forest, it seeks to endow itself with novelty in order to create the mobile and overexcited spectacle of the city; but that powerful African pedal note in the first chapters evidently needed a larger symphony to be developed upon it. It was, probably, in the poet's spirit; he did not have the patience to unfold it because of the overwhelming movement that typifies and at times impairs his genius.

Silvio Benco

*

Marinetti's Response to Benco
(in Bruno Sanzin, *Marinetti e il Futurismo*,
Trieste, 1924, pp. 29-31)

Dear Benco,

The praise that you have devoted to my most recent book, *The Untameables*, convinces me that the meaning of this work has, in part, escaped you.

First of all, I do not see what connection could exist between Wells and myself. Comparing me to Wells is the same as comparing Victor Hugo to Jules Verne. Like Jules Verne, Wells is entirely devoid of lyricism, incapable of giving a plastic coloristic and musical life to his characters and landscapes. The characters and language of their books are indistinct often confused always banal, never animated by true artistic life.

I start with freshly created images. These qualities make me seem obscure to readers of Wells and pleasing to those who generally do not care for Wells.

For example, the 3 Governing Paper People: Notnor the reactionary denier of freedom, Yessir the wise ex-

ploiter and classifier of freedom and Well...the oscillating doubt in method and philosophy. These 3 characters are three political concepts and they are also
three lyrical syntheses. Therefore they are part of the
pure poetic creation and have nothing to do with the
amusing formula of the adventure novel.

I will now clarify the philosophic-symbolic meaning
of *The Untameables* by quoting the exact words of a
highly intelligent friend of mine: over the untamed ferocity (of the Untameables) is the less crude ferocity of
the Negro Jailers, a ferocity which is guided and exploited. Both are instinctive, primordial, cruel, unconscious forces.

Above them are the Paper People, symbols of ideas
and hence of the Book which nails down but does not
tame the instincts. They drown themselves only in the
calm even light of the Lake of Goodness that annihi-
lates diversity, destroys harshness, lights up wounds,
enhances torment-sin. But in the Lake of Goodness the
ferocious humans become happy and luminous, yet they
do not remain there. Humans find no truth in immobility even when it is happy immobility, nor do they find
truth in unconsciousness even when it is divine.

The Untameables emerge from Feeling to enter the
kingdom of ideas, the life of the spirit, the life of ab-
stract constructions. On the other hand the luminous
and dynamic abstractions rise over reality, and it is the
uniform opaque and sad mass of the workers that holds

them up high. They work, and because of the same general dynamism of the Forces they submit to work, still wishing for the ideal product of their atrocious labor. Their poor wish is already thoughtful and projects them into the great marvelous Lake of Poetry. A lake that is creation become reality.

They rebel against the rhythm imposed by the brain that demands their submissive work, and they want to reach the eternal and pure rhythm of constructed feeling. The tamed instincts of the Untameables break loose and aid the Untamed River People. This is how the Forces transpose and transmit themselves, without anymore limitations, since clear-cut divisions are absurd.

Only the ferocity, cruelty, destruction which were tame yesterday can be today a conscious and willful guide to the future. But the forces which were tamed for an instant unleash themselves and are once more anarchic, individualistic, ferocious. Again they become unconscious, brutal, and criminal instincts that must be chained up. And everything would return to its original state. But Humans possess the continuity of consciousness.

Thus from the book arises the synthesis of the individual-man in his striving toward the emotional fullness that overflows into cerebral life. This life sometimes becomes tyrannical and it exploits the material forces that it once tried to surpass.

And the synthesis of the individual-society arises

ing for progress. A striving toward a broth-
most achieved, enlightened by ideas, but
y the burning heat of the same ideas that in-
ce again its dense and opaque elements.

And the synthesis of Humanity arises.

Humanity aching in its anguished mystery, with none
of its thirsts ever satisfied, its burning thirst always
exacerbated. Humanity thirsting for a truth that embraces, floods, and caresses. The only truth, the only
force: Goodness. Absolute goodness without any reser-
vations, without any spasms. Goodness of the soul that
finds itself in other souls and rests content with this
finding free of possession. But goodness is not enough
for human vitality. Humanity is dynamic, constructive.
It believes in construction, it wills the creation that is
its future.

F. T. Marinetti

F.T. MARINETTI

Born in Alexandria, Egypt in 1876, Filippo Tommaso Marinetti spent his early youth in Paris, culminating in his taking a degree at the Sorbonne. In the years following, he returned to his parents' home of Italy, attending the University of Pavia and graduating from the law school of the University of Genoa.

His earliest writings were in French, including a long epic poem, *La conquête des étoiles* (1902), a portrait of the Italian decadent writer Gabrielle D'Annunzio in 1903, and lyric poems (*Poèmes lyriques*) in 1904. The following year Marinetti moved to Milan, where he founded an international journal of poetry *Poesia*, committed primarily to French Symbolism. However, the journal also published the work of younger Italian poets, and it was with these poets that Marinetti organized his "poètes incendiaires," the roots of his Futurist movement. The same year Marinetti published his Alfred Jarry-influenced *Le Roi Bombance*.

By 1909 Marinetti had defined his aesthetics sufficiently to produce the "Manifeste du Futurisme" in the French newspaper *Le Figaro*; he republished his first Futurist manifesto the same year in *Poesia*. Several other major manifestos followed over the next few years, and along with these Marinetti produced other "syntheses" and theatrical writings of which critic Marjorie Perloff has described as "…incomparable, the strategy of his manifestos, performances, recitations, and fictions being to transform politics into a kind of lyric theater." Casting his manifestos into a narrative framework that was grounded in Symbolist images, Marinetti nonetheless rushed his language forward in a whirl of theatrical devices which dynamized and radicalized his discourse.

The themes of Marinetti's writings—energy, audacity, aggressiveness, violence, and heroism—were not so much the basis of a coherent system of thought as they were forces for a rejection of the old, of the static and diluted conventions of late nineteenth century art and life. Marinetti's Futurism—like the Russian Constructivism and Futurism, the French Cubism, and the English Vorticism—brought art into the industrialized and mechanized world which the late Romantics, many Victorians, and Decadents had sought to escape.

Marinetti's art is at once aestheticized and brutal, rhetorically sophisticated and politically naive, contradictions which led Marinetti—as it did many modernists, including the Vorticist Ezra Pound and Marinetti's admirer D.H. Lawrence—to embrace Fascism, which under Mussolini shared similar positions in relation to heroism, violence and the new.

Marinetti's legacy, however, lies not in his political involvements or theories, but in the forging of poetic and performative genres (such as his manifestos and "syntheses") that are equally (perhaps more) at home in postmodern culture.

Marinetti died on December 2, 1944 in Bellagio.

SUN & MOON CLASSICS

This publication was made possible, in part, through an operational grant from the Andrew W. Mellon Foundation and through contributions from the following individuals:

Charles Altieri (Seattle, Washington)
John Arden (Galway, Ireland)
Jesse Huntley Ausubel (New York, New York)
Dennis Barone (West Hartford, Connecticut)
Jonathan Baumbach (Brooklyn, New York)
Guy Bennett (Los Angeles, California)
Bill Berkson (Bolinas, California)
Steve Benson (Berkeley, California)
Charles Bernstein and Susan Bee (New York, New York)
Dorothy Bilik (Silver Spring, Maryland)
José Camillo Cela (in memorium)
Bill Corbett (Boston, Massachusetts)
Fielding Dawson (New York, New York)
Robert Crosson (Los Angeles, California)
Tina Darragh and P. Inman (Greenbelt, Maryland)
Christopher Dewdney (Toronto, Canada)
George Economou (Norman, Oklahoma)
Elaine Equi and Jerome Sala (New York, New York)
Lawrence Ferlinghetti (San Francisco, California)
Richard Foreman (New York, New York)
Howard N. Fox (Los Angeles, California)
Jerry Fox (Aventura, Florida)
In Memoriam: Rose Fox
Melvyn Freilicher (San Diego, California)
Miro Gavran (Zagreb, Croatia)
Peter Glassgold (Brooklyn, New York)
Barbara Guest (New York, New York)
Perla and Amiram V. Karney (Bel Air, California)
Fred Haines (Los Angeles, California)
Václav Havel (Prague, The Czech Republic)
Fanny Howe (La Jolla, California)
Harold Jaffe (San Diego, California)
Ira S. Jaffe (Albuquerque, New Mexico)
Alex Katz (New York, New York)
Tom LaFarge (New York, New York)

Mary Jane Lafferty (Los Angeles, California)
Michael Lally (Santa Monica, California)
Norman Lavers (Jonesboro, Arkansas)
Jerome Lawrence (Malibu, California)
Stacey Levine (Seattle, Washington)
Herbert Lust (Greenwich, Connecticut)
Norman MacAffee (New York, New York)
Rosemary Macchiavelli (Washington, DC)
Beatrice Manley (Los Angeles, California)
Martin Nakell (Los Angeles, California)
Toby Olson (Philadelphia, Pennsylvania)
Maggie O'Sullivan (Hebden Bridge, England)
Rochelle Owens (Norman, Oklahoma)
Marjorie and Joseph Perloff (Pacific Palisades, California)
Dennis Phillips (Los Angeles, California)
Carl Rakosi (San Francisco, California)
David Reed (New York, New York)
Ishmael Reed (Oakland, California)
Janet Rodney (Santa Fe, New Mexico)
Joe Ross (Washington, DC)
Dr. Marvin and Ruth Sackner (Miami Beach, Florida)
Floyd Salas (Berkeley, California)
Tom Savage (New York, New York)
Leslie Scalapino (Oakland, California)
James Sherry (New York, New York)
Aaron Shurin (San Francisco, California)
Charles Simic (Strafford, New Hampshire)
Gilbert Sorrentino (Stanford, California)
Catharine R. Stimpson (Staten Island, New York)
John Taggart (Newburg, Pennsylvania)
Nathaniel Tarn (Tesuque, New Mexico)
Fiona Templeton (New York, New York)
Mitch Tuchman (Los Angeles, California)
Hannah Walker and Ceacil Eisner (Orlando, Florida)
Wendy Walker (New York, New York)
Anne Walter (Carnac, France)
Arnold Wesker (Hay on Wye, England)

If you would like to be a contributor to this series, please send your tax-deductible contribution to The Contemporary Arts Educational Project, Inc., a non-profit corporation, 6026 Wilshire Boulevard,Los Angeles, California 90036.

RECENT BOOKS IN THE SUN & MOON CLASSICS

*First American publication

**Revised edition